The Cowboy and His Vegas Wedding

Cowboys of Rock Springs, Texas #3

Kaci M. Rose

Five Little Roses Publishing

Copyright

Book Cover By: **Sweet 'N Spicy Designs**

Editing By: Debbe @ **On the Page, Author and PA Services**

Proofread By: Nikki @ **Southern Sweetheart Services**

Blurb

Viva Las Vegas! Wedding bells are ringing for Rock Springs... Sin City style!

Anna Mae

To say I have little trust in men is an understatement. After I caught my husband cheating with his secretary, and he ended our marriage, I swore never to be blinded by love again. I've noticed Royce around for over a year now and can't deny the hot rush of heat I feel, whenever our gazes meet. Still, I don't trust myself enough to allow it to be more than a casual flirtation. We may both be headed to a bachelor/bachelorette party in Las Vegas, but I'm completely confident I can keep my libido in check. I mean, what's the worst that could happen?

Royce

Drinks were flowing, as we celebrated my sister and her fiancé's upcoming wedding. Next thing I know, I'm waking up in bed with Anna Mae, and it seems we did a whole lot more than spend the night together. Our drunken selves found a cute, little chapel and tied the knot. Anna is understandably upset, but I see this as an opportunity with a beautiful woman I genuinely care for. Can I convince her to take a gamble on our happily ever after? Or once we are back in Rock Springs, will we roll snake eyes on what could have been a beautiful future?

Dedication

To the coffee that kept me going, and the kids that call me mommy.

Contents

Get Free Books!

Would you like some free cowboy books?
**If you join Kaci M. Rose's Newsletter you
get books and bonus epilogues free!
Join Kaci M. Rose's newsletter and get
your free books!**
https://www.kacirose.com/KMR-Newsletter

Now on to the story!

Prologue

Royce

1 Year Ago

I can see Ella fitting in here in Rock Springs. She and Jason have started courting, and today, he's giving us a tour around town. Rock Springs is smaller than our home of Mountain Gap, Tennessee, but I like the people here a whole lot better. It's a ranching town, and the cowboys seem to be the best neighbors you could ask for.

We walk into the beauty salon that Jason's sister, Megan, owns. I know Ella is excited to see it because she loves to do other people's hair. She's always in high demand for weddings at the church.

From what little I know of Megan, the beauty salon fits her. It's not too girly and still has the cowboy style. It's what my sister calls farmhouse decor. If you take out the smell of hair dye, it wouldn't be a bad place for the men in town to hang out either. Though looking around, I don't see a single male here other than my dad and myself.

Laughter comes from the back corner, and my heart stops. Something about that laugh draws me in to get closer, to see where it's coming from. That's when I see her. This stunning woman, doing the lady's hair in the back corner, is laughing, and it sounds like magic.

My feet pull me towards her without me even realizing it, and it's just my luck the lady whose hair she was doing gets up and heads to check out. She starts cleaning up her station, as I reach her.

"Hello, I'm Royce," I say to her.

She pauses, looks at me, and smiles hesitantly.

"I'm Anna Mae." Her southern accent drawls, and just like her laugh, it's calming, and I know I'd do just about anything to hear her talk.

"My sister, Ella, is dating Megan's brother, Jason," I tell her to explain why some strange man randomly walked up to her in a beauty shop. Her eyes dart over to where Megan is talking with my parents, my sister, Maggie, Ella, and Jason.

"Megan said you are from Dallas?" I try to get her to talk.

This must have been the wrong thing to say because her eyes storm over.

"I moved here from Dallas, yes, but I'm from the Austin area. Came to stay with my grandma for a bit." She keeps sweeping the floor.

I rack my brain for what the reason for moving from Dallas is, but I can't for the life of me remember.

"Didn't like the big city?" I ask hesitantly, hoping she will fill in the blanks.

"I didn't mind it until I walked in to find my husband fucking his secretary, and of course, she wound up pregnant, before I could get out of town. So now, I don't like big cities so much." She stops sweeping and levels me with a glare that I'm guessing is supposed to scare me, but all I can focus on is one word. *Husband.*

"Still married?" I croak out.

"Nope, but don't bother asking me out. Royce, as far as I'm concerned, all you men are assholes, and I'm not giving away my trust anytime soon."

I can't help but smile this time. Bigger than I remember smiling before.

"Challenge accepted. I'll be here Anna Mae for as long as it takes. You'll have to talk to Megan. I'm not like the other guys around here."

She grunts and tries to pretend to ignore me, as she finishes sweeping the hair up from around her chair, but I see her giving me the side-eye.

"See you real soon, sweet Anna Mae," I say and turn to walk back over to my family.

I think my family's style of courting might appeal to her. No unchaperoned dates. No sex or even kissing, until you're married. She's very skittish and has every right to be. This might work in my favor.

The look on my dad's face says he knows exactly what just happened. I make a mental note to talk to Megan tonight and find out everything I can on my sweet Anna Mae because I'm going to need everything I can to win her over.

Chapter 1

Royce

How can my head hurt so much, and I haven't even opened my eyes yet today? It feels like a rock band has been practicing all night and has no plans of stopping. What did I do last night to cause this?

I groan, opening my eyes slowly, and I realize I'm not in my bed. It takes a minute before I realize I'm in a hotel room. A hotel room in Las Vegas for my sister Maggie and her fiancé Nick's joint bachelor and bachelorette parties.

I shut my eyes again and turn my back to the window, and that's when I feel the sheet on me and realize that I'm naked. I never sleep naked. What the hell happened last night?

I remember last night we went to a circus show that Maggie has been going on about for days. What I remember was good. Then again, add a trained tiger to any show, and it will catch most guys' attention. Everyone was there and having fun. My parents, Maggie, Nick, Nick's parents, Ella and Jason, Jason's family, including his parents, Blaze and Riley, Sage and Colt, Megan and Hunter, and Mac and Sarah. As promised, Anna Mae's grandma, Mrs. Willow, was there and got Anna Mae to come, too. Baby Lilly, Blaze, and Riley's daughter are staying with Lilly and Mike in Rock Springs for the weekend.

I remember Sage and Colt ordered a drink called a fishbowl. It was blue and had swimming gummy fishes in it. It was more than enough for two people. Mrs. Willow ordered one for Anna Mae and me. She kept encouraging us to drink, and I convinced Anna Mae to drink it with me. I didn't taste any alcohol in it, but it had to have some with the way my head feels. How many did we drink? Three? Four? More? I don't know.

What happened after the show? I have small flashes of our group walking down The Strip back to our hotel. Maybe, that's it? No, I remember my parents and Jason's parents saying good night and going to bed, but we all were staying up a bit longer. I remember being shocked that Mrs. Willow was keeping up with us.

Where did we go next? I think Mrs. Willow was going to show us something Elvis related. It's all a blur after that. My head is still pounding, as I grip my forehead, willing it to stop when I freeze, as cold metal hits my skin.

I pull my hand back and crack open my eyes. It's a ring. On my ring finger. On my left hand.

What the hell happened last night? When I feel someone else shift in bed next to me, I about jump out of my skin. I look over to see Anna Mae next to me. She looks so calm and peaceful sleeping. I could stare at her all day. My brain keeps pulling me back, saying we have to figure this out before she wakes up because she will demand answers.

A quick peek under the sheets confirms she's naked too, and I can't tear my eyes away. She has her back to me, and her smooth skin is begging to be touched, her long, brown hair spread out on her pillow. The curve of her back and the round globes of her ass have me getting hard, which would not be a great way for her to wake up and find me.

I put the sheet down and run my eyes over her, and I don't think I've seen a more beautiful sight. I've never seen a woman first thing in the morning with their defenses down other than my sisters and my mom, so I soak up this moment. Then, I see the ring on her left hand. The one that matches mine.

There's no way we went and got married in Vegas, right? But it makes sense. The rings and us naked in bed. I don't even remember my wedding night. Hell, even worse, I lost my virginity, and I don't even remember it.

I start looking around the room. Clothes are everywhere, and on the nightstand next to Anna Mae, is a marriage certificate from The Elvis Wedding Chapel. This has Mrs. Willow written all over it. I wonder if she planned this. I know she has been on my side for months, trying to get Anna Mae to move on from her ex, but even this is a bit crazy.

I collapse back on the bed and dig the heels of my palms into my eyes. This can't be happening.

As Anna Mae starts to stir, my whole body stiffens, as I wait for her to realize I'm here. I turn my head to look at her, watching this beautiful woman wake up.

She turns on to her back groaning, and I'm guessing her head hurts, as much as mine does. As she turns, the sheet falls below her chest. I know I should turn away, but her perfect breasts are on full display, and I can't convince myself to turn my head. Even as I feel myself getting hard again, my eyes rake over them.

When she groans again, it breaks the spell. I look up towards the ceiling and close my eyes, deciding to make myself known.

"You should drink some water," I say.

She screams and jumps out of bed, taking the sheet with her, leaving me on full display. I don't move, because I want her to get her bearings.

"Royce?!" She asks in a shriek that the rock band in my head doesn't like very much.

Then, she realizes what she did. While she's fully covered with the sheet, I am not. She freezes, and her eyes rake down my body in all its glory. The longer she looks, the harder I get, and I don't try to stop it. I know the moment her eyes see my cock, because her whole body flushes the most beautiful pink. It makes my cock jump, and that's enough to snap her out of it.

"Why are you in my room?" She asks.

I chuckle and sit up with my back to the headboard.

"Sweet Anna, you're in my room." I nod towards where my bags are on the chair.

She looks around, and then her eyes land on the marriage certificate, and she walks slowly towards it like it might jump up and bite her.

"No..." She says and sits on the edge of the bed with the paper in her hands. Her hands shake, and all I want to do, is reach out and hold her, but I don't think she would take kindly to that.

"Seems so," I say, as I take her pillow and cover my lap, more for her sake than mine.

"We're married?" She whispers.

"Well, I'm not sure I remember any more about last night than you. I remember mine and Jason's parents going to bed..."

She finishes the memory, "And my grandma saying something about Elvis."

"Yep, then a whole lot of nothing. I woke up just minutes before you and put the pieces together."

She looks over her shoulder at me "Did we..." Her face flushes a nice shade of pink.

"I don't know, sweetheart. I want to say I hope not, because it would suck not to remember my first time."

"Our first time?" She tries to correct me. While I never flat out admitted to Anna Mae that I'm a virgin, well at least I was, until last night, I did dance around the subject, hoping she'd catch on.

"That too, but it would have been my first time." I look her in the eyes, willing her to understand. The moment it clicks, understanding crosses her face.

I stand up and pull on my boxers that were thankfully on the floor by the bed. Then, I walk over and kneel in front of her. Her eyes follow me, and something in my chest clicks into place. She's my wife, and she's mine.

I place a hand on her cheek, and she leans into me. I know I had my first kiss last night at our wedding, but this morning, I want one I will remember. I lean in slowly, so she knows what's happening. When she bends towards me, relief washes over me.

My lips touch hers, and it's nothing like I always thought my first kiss would me. Her lips are warm and soft against mine with just a hint of that strawberry Chapstick she's always wearing. My body warms all over like this kiss is filling my soul full of her.

I pull back much sooner than I want to, but I don't want to push her too far too fast either. I pull back just enough to be able to look into her eyes and see the scared look is gone. I soak in this moment and pray it can last forever.

Then, our phones go off at the same time. I reach for mine on the nightstand and see it's the group text from Megan.

Megan: Good Morning! Everyone to the buffet. We have two sets of newlyweds to celebrate!

"No. No, no, no, no," Anna Mae says and starts pacing the room. "They all know. I can't be married. We can get this annulled. We can fix this." She's saying this more to herself, as she clutches the sheet tighter to her chest.

Something about how she's so dead set on not being married, makes me snap.

"You know, at some point, you're going to have to understand I'm not your ex. I don't know what else I have to do to prove it. You keep pushing me away, and yet, here I am. I'm still here, and I'm not going anywhere. I'm not him, and it's not fair that you keep treating me like him. And I'm not agreeing to an annulment, wife."

I don't give her a chance to respond, as I head into the bathroom and walk right into the shower. The cold water hits me, like a punishment for what happened last night, or for my harsh words to Anna Mae just now.

As the water warms, I try to remember more of last night, but nothing comes to me. I make a mental note to check my phone to see if by chance there are some photos or texts from last night.

Then, I think of Anna Mae. There's no way I'm giving up on this marriage. This is what I have been working on for a year now. We are married, and I need to convince her to give it and me a real chance. Maybe, if she can give me a year and we truly work on our marriage, I know I can prove to her how great we can be together. She just needs to open up to me and stop pushing me away.

I love this woman with all my heart, and the distance she keeps between us is killing me. Waking up today and finding out she's my wife, it's like something clicked into place. I'm not walking away from this. and I won't let her either.

I wash up and dry off. When I come out of the bathroom with the towel around my waist, she's gone as are her clothes. My guess is she went to her room down the hall to get a shower and get dressed for breakfast.

I get dressed and ready to head out. Checking my phone, there's not a single thing from last night. I send up a prayer of thanks that Megan is pregnant, so I know she wasn't drinking, as I'm sure most of the guys weren't either, because they would want to make sure their wives were okay. Maybe, someone can fill in the blanks for me at breakfast.

Chapter 2

Anna Mae

I close the door to my room and collapse against it.

What have I done?

Grandma always says that what you do when you're drunk is what you want to do, but stop yourself from doing, while you're sober.

I don't think she could have hit the nail more on the head if she tried. How many nights have I stayed up and dreamed of the life Royce and I could have? How many times did I stay up trying to remind myself of why I can't have that life again?

I can't become vulnerable like that again. To give someone that kind of trust and open myself up to that kind of pain again. I just can't do it. It almost killed me last time, and it took every last bit of willpower I had left to scrape up the pieces and move on. It took everything out of me to get back on my own two feet.

I never thought Liam was the kind of man who would cheat on me with his secretary, get the girl pregnant, and leave me.

There's a voice in the back of my head, reminding me Royce isn't like that. He's sweet and kind and has been here for me the last year, asking nothing in return. Liam wouldn't have lasted a month.

I head into the shower and let the warm water soothe away my worries. Of course, there were warning signs with Liam. He didn't talk to his family. In the six years we were together, I never met his parents or anyone outside his Dallas circle. My family didn't like him, but they tried for me. His temper was short with everyone but me.

Compared to Royce, well, his family is some of the nicest people I know. Megan talks about them all the time. My grandma adores Royce, and I've never once seen Royce lose control of his temper, even in situations that I know Liam would.

I can't believe I drank so much last night. The hot water loosens up all my tense muscles. What the heck happened last night? The image of Royce naked on the bed this morning flashes in my head, and I can't deny he has an amazing body. Mix that with his just woken up look with his light brown, curly hair a mess, and my head has plenty of ideas for how I would definitely take that for a ride.

These thoughts are only turning me on, and I don't have time to deal with that, because we are expected downstairs. I quickly wash my hair and the rest of me, before getting out and getting dressed. I go for more comfortable today, because I know we are hitting some casinos and taking in the strip if the plans haven't changed.

I gather my stuff and nearly jump out of my skin, as I walk into the hallway and find Royce, leaning against my door. I give him my best what the fuck look, as I close the door behind me.

"If you think I'm going to let my wife walk around Las Vegas alone where anything can happen to her, you best think again." He says as we walk towards the elevator.

"Great," I say under my breath. He pushes the button to head downstairs and then turns back to me.

"You may not like it, but you're my wife, and that means something to me. I will make sure you're okay and protected. I won't let you fend for yourself. I will take care of you, even if you fight me on it." His lip tilts up just a bit in the corner, like the idea of me fighting him on it is amusing.

We get in the elevator, and it's just us in the confined space, and he doesn't give me my space here either. He stands so close to me that I can feel his body heat. We don't say a word on the way down to the lobby. The moment the elevator door opens it's a whirlwind of activity with the sounds from the casino, and the smell from the buffet all filling the air.

Royce takes my hand and guides me to where we are meeting his family. They are towards the back of the restaurant, so they have plenty of time to take us in, as we make our way to where they are taking up five tables in the back.

Of course, we are the last ones there, so the last seats are right next to each other. Royce, ever the gentleman, pulls out my chair and pushes me in. Then, he takes his seat next to me, and I don't miss him scooting his chair closer to me. Neither does my grandma, who winks at me. I don't smile at her, because I'm pretty sure she has something to do with my mysterious wedding.

Royce leans into my ear, "Just go along with them today and make this a good day for Maggie and Nick, please. This should be about them. We'll talk tonight."

He's right; after all, we are here to celebrate Maggie and Nick. The fact he doesn't want to take away from them shows the love he has for his family, and proves once again, how different he is from Liam.

"To the newlyweds!" Sage cheers and everyone looks our way and raises their glasses. I feel the heat creep up my face, but Royce is right there to step in.

"Thank you, guys. At some point, someone will have to share photos or recap the night to us." He laughs. "Now, you said two newlyweds?"

Sage waves her hand "Oh, Maggie and Nick are as good as married. Now, go get something to eat."

We head to the massive buffet that claims to have over two-hundred items on the buffet. Royce is right by my side the whole way. He helps carry my plates and is patient, as I walk to each station to see what there is.

"I like how you take a little bit of everything you want to try. It's cute." He smiles at me, and my heart skips a beat. Liam would have been so frustrated that he'd already be sitting down and eating his meal. This is all new, that has to be it. He can't be like this all the time, right?

He's acting like this morning never happened. Like I didn't freak out and basically ask to end our marriage, before it even started. I know he said we will talk about it later, but it's on my mind now and will be all day.

We head back to the table, and he makes sure I'm all situated and have everything I need. He takes note of how I take my coffee and which items I liked and which I didn't. There's something more in his eyes, a gleam in those dark brown eyes. I can't seem to place it, but it's almost like he's happy to do all these things and happy to take care of me. Could he really be?

After breakfast, we spend the day casino hopping. This was my grandma's idea, and everyone jumped on board.

We are on our fourth casino of the day, and this one has a circus theme. Half the group is gambling here and there, and the other half is taking in the sites and shops at each place. My grandma is playing the tables like it's a sport.

Royce is by my side the whole time. He carries my bags, gets me drinks, and has taken dozens of photos. He's tried his hand at a few slots when I insisted. I've also watched him check up on his sisters and his mom too, even though, they have guys of their own to watch out for them. I love that he still cares enough to make sure they are okay.

Right before dinner, my grandma walks up and shoos Royce away. He falls in step behind us; I'm guessing, so he can keep an eye on me.

"That husband of yours hasn't left your side at all today," Grandma says with a twinkle in her eye.

"Probably scared I'll run away, and he won't see me again," I say sarcastically.

"Oh, pish. That boy is head over heels for you, and everyone but you can see it. I'm happy for you two, and I just ask you give it a real chance. Don't dismiss it, because of how it happened."

"Grandma, I'm starting to think you had something to do with this."

"Who, me?" She says with a sparkle in her eye and then starts power walking to catch up with Royce's parents.

After dinner, we leave to catch a night showing of The Bellagio water fountain show. It lights up with all different colors, as Royce stands behind me with his hands lightly on my hips. It makes me smile because it's simple and easy. My body also wastes no time telling me how much it likes his hands on me. As he rubs slow circles over my shirt, it turns me on more and more. I'm thankful when the show ends, and I can take a step away.

Thanks to him, this has been an amazing day. It's nice to have someone else on your team. It's the little things, like holding your purse, when you go to the restroom, or getting you a drink, so you don't lose the good slot machine.

I don't even realize I'm leaning back against him until he wraps his arms around my waist and places his head next to mine.

"This is my favorite part of the day." He whispers.

I turn my head to whisper back. "Darn, I thought it would have been waking up in bed naked with me." I joke.

His eyes heat over, and he pulls me back into him more, so I can feel his hard length against my ass.

"Of course, I loved that, but you were pulling away from me then. Now, you're leaning into me. That makes this so much better."

A pang of guilt hits me. Did he really admit to me that he was a virgin, or maybe, he still is? He had talked a little, but I just thought he was inexperienced, or maybe, lost it at prom and had only been with one girl. But a virgin? And why does the thought of him being with no one but me, turn me on so much?

"Will you think about something for me?" He asks, pulling me from my thoughts.

"What is it?" I ask.

"Will you consider moving your stuff into my room? We are married, and it will be expected of..."

"I will." Comes out of my mouth, before I can think twice.

He looks as shocked as I feel, but the dread I wait to wash over me never comes.

We walk back to our hotel with the group and say our goodnights. My grandma comes over and hugs me tight, whispering in my ear.

"Remember what I said, you give this a chance. It's still a marriage in the eyes of God, even if you were married by Elvis." She smirks at me.

"Grandma!" I gasp. "I knew it!"

"You can't prove it!" She hollers over her shoulder, as she heads to catch the elevator.

Royce walks up beside me and watches her go, before looking back at me. "Let's go get your stuff, so we can talk a bit."

Once in my room, he helps me pack my stuff and carry it back to his. Once there, he sets my stuff down and takes my hand, leading me to the couch. He doesn't let go of my hand, even once we are seated.

"I just bought a place right outside of town. It's not a huge place only about fifty acres, but the house has four bedrooms. I want to make this work and for you to give this marriage a real chance. I don't want an answer from you now. I want you to think about it. You can have your own space at the house. I don't expect you to jump into bed with me. Even tonight, you take the bed, and I'll take the couch."

Can I do this without opening up and making myself vulnerable again? He deserves a chance, even if I can't give him all of me.

"I promise to think about it and give you an answer before we leave Vegas."

His smile is blinding, as he pulls me in for a hug. A hug that is more comforting than it should be. I have three more days to figure out what I'm going to do.

Chapter 3

Royce

Tonight, we are going to a concert. Maggie and Nick wanted to see it, but they won't tell us who it is. They just promised we'd all enjoy it. I guess it's one of the cleaner shows. I've noticed from the signs most of the shows the people have minimal clothes on, but hey, that's Vegas, right?

Anna Mae is getting ready in the bathroom, so I sit on the couch, thinking of the conversation I had with my parents yesterday. They pulled me aside at one of the casinos. I had been dreading the conversation, but they surprised me.

My dad asked if I wanted this, and I told him more than anything. Of course, I'd rather it happened another way, but I told them that I was going to fight to make it work. Then, he smiled, saying they support me 100%. They also want to throw a small reception for us and let everyone be part of it when we get home. I promised to talk to Anna Mae, and I will, but I want her to agree to move in with me first.

I'm still unclear of what happened the night we got married. Everyone seems to be a bit tight-lipped, but Anna Mae thinks her grandma was behind it and given the Elvis theme to it all, I have to agree. One day when we get home, I need to take her to lunch again and get the details from her.

When the door opens, and Anna Mae walks out, I swallow my tongue. She looks like an angel with the light from the bathroom, shining behind her. Her long hair is up in a beautiful bun with her bangs braided and pulled back into it. She's in a tan dress that falls to her knees and has lace on the edges and a brown leather belt around her waist. My favorite part? She's rocking her brown cowboy boots. She looks every bit like the cowboy's wife she now is.

"Damn, Anna Mae. You look stunning. I'm not going to be able to let you out of my sight tonight, because every guy will be lining up to talk to you." I say, as I cross the room and take her hands in mine.

She looks at her feet, as a light blush stains her cheeks. I have noticed she doesn't take compliments very well, but that doesn't mean I'm going to stop. I kiss her cheek, and we head downstairs to meet up with everyone else in the lobby.

As we leave the elevator, she reaches for my hand. It's such a small thing, but it means a lot to me.

"Any idea what show we are going to go see?" Riley asks.

"No clue. They have been so secretive," Sage says, as we all look around for Maggie and Nick, who are the only ones missing now.

A moment later the elevator opens, and they walk out with huge smiles on their faces.

"Oh, good. We are all here! Let's go!" Maggie says.

She and Nick lead the way, and it looks like the show is here in the hotel. I rack my brain for the show posters I've seen, but I haven't paid much attention.

"Any idea what show it is here at the hotel?" I ask Anna Mae.

"No, I'm not sure."

"Me either, but it looks like they got us some good seats," I say, as we head towards the front of the stage and are seated just a few rows away from the front row.

We take up a whole row, which is saying something, because this place is huge, and so are the rows, and there are nineteen of us here. Once we are all settled, everyone's phones go off, and it's a text from Maggie.

Maggie: I got a call from Lilly last night, and she helped set this up.

Since Blaze is sitting next to me, I look over at his wife, Riley, who is Lilly's best friend, and who is also watching their daughter this weekend.

"Any idea what she's talking about?" I ask her.

"No clue. Lilly hasn't said anything to me." She shrugs.

It isn't long before her cryptic message makes sense. The opening act takes the stage, and it's Savannah, Lilly's sister. She's starting a tour with a band called The 3 Stevens soon.

"I thought she was touring on the East Coast!" Anna Mae says in my ear.

Almost like Maggie was expecting the questions, we all get a text.

Maggie: They got this spot last minute because the other act canceled. Lilly called me to arrange the surprise.

Our whole group is on our feet, and the girls are yelling support to Savannah, who's waving at us. She's a talented performer and has the entire crowd energized.

Anna Mae is up, and by the time The 3 Stevens take the stage, she's in my arms, her back to my front, and my arms around her waist. I send up a silent prayer for many more nights like this with her in my arms. She seems to be letting her guard down, and I'm loving every minute of it.

As soon as the concert is over, we all pile into the lobby, and Riley calls Lilly.

"Lilly! You should have been here! We could have made it happen!" Riley is still pumped up from the show, and it shows in her voice.

"And give up a weekend of solid baby time? No way! Besides, I have some dates planned to go see her with my parents, during the tour." Lilly Laughs.

Riley named her daughter after Lilly, who saved her life and brought her to Blaze, which started the chain of events that led to Ella meeting Jason and me meeting Anna Mae.

When Blaze and Riley named their little girl after her, it was emotional for all of us. She loves on that little girl as if she was her own, and I know they will have a special bond, as she grows up. The baby is already spoiled, and she's not even four months old yet.

"Well, I sent you a bunch of photos and a video, so make sure to send them on to your parents, too. We're all going to bed, but thank you for this!" Riley says with a huge smile on her face.

"Oh, Mike was over at the ranch today, and everything is going well. Jenna's brothers are doing great." Lilly says.

Sarah's friend, Jenna, has three brothers, who are looking to buy a ranch in the next few years. They have a lot of experience, and when we started trying to figure out the logistics of all the couples coming to Vegas for the weekend, Sarah suggested they come out and pitch in. I guess, they jumped at the chance to do so.

Riley and Lilly talk a bit more before they say goodbye.

"Okay, you guys have fun and stay safe. See you in a few days." Lilly says, and we all say goodbye.

"See you all at breakfast tomorrow," Ella says and winks at me. I have a plan up my sleeve, and she and my parents are in on it.

We go our separate ways, and once back in our room, I decide it's now or never to talk to Anna Mae.

"So, have you thought about moving in with me?" I ask. I don't want to push, but I'm desperate to know.

She sighs and looks undecided, so I keep talking.

"Because the thing is, I'm willing to do just about anything to make this work." I look her right in the eyes and hit her with the next one. "I love you, Anna Mae."

She sucks in a breath, so I keep going.

"We can decide how we move forward. Maybe, we can just go on dates and get to know each other more. You moving in, is me taking care of you, as my wife. I will do that no matter what, and no matter how hard you push me away. Tomorrow, we are going on a honeymoon, and I've already cleared it with the family. Just you and me. I have the whole day planned."

Her eyes never leave mine, but I can't read the expression on her face.

"Royce, what if we..." She pauses and looks out of the window, gathering her words, and I give her the time she needs.

"What if we keep it casual, like friends with benefits?"

I hate the idea of her thinking we are just friends. We are so much more, and I will prove that to her in time. But this is a step in the right direction, and maybe after tomorrow, she will loosen up more.

"I can agree to that if you'll move in with me. You can have your own room on the other end of the house. Heck, you can even take two rooms. Just move in and let me take care of my wife." I almost sound like I'm pleading, and maybe I am.

"Okay." She whispers, and the relief and excitement that hit me at the same time are overwhelming. Before I know it, I have her in my arms, and when she melts against me, I know we have a fighting chance.

"Let's get ready for bed, and then I'll let you ask me any questions you want, and I'll answer them," I tell her. I want her to get to know me, and I hope in turn I will get to know her.

"Okay. I guess fair is fair, but only one question, and my ex is off-limits. I'm not ready to go down that rabbit hole." She says as she gathers her clothes. I nod and watch her walk to the bathroom. When she closes the door, it's like a trance is broken, and I rush into action to get changed, thinking about my question.

I want to ask something that will let me get to know her more, and I know exactly what my question will be. When she comes out of the bathroom, I take my turn to get ready as quickly as possible and then join her on the couch.

She turns sideways to face me, pulling her legs up in front of her. "You go first." She says to me.

I take her hand for a little connection to give her strength, but also, her touch calms me.

"I know you enjoy doing hair, but if you could do anything, no concern for people or money. What would it be?" I ask her.

I want to be a part of making her dreams come true. I will work my butt off to make sure it happens, too.

"As in a job? I've always wanted to do hair. I was always doing the girls' hair on the playground as a kid, and my mom's hair growing up. Anyone who would let me." She shrugs, and I get a feeling this isn't the whole answer. I narrow my eyes when she looks up at me.

"It doesn't have to be a job, my sweet girl," I say, and her eyes go wide. I'm learning to read when she's holding back, and before, I would let her do it, too. Now that she's my wife, I plan to push her a bit more.

"Well, it doesn't matter, because it won't happen now." She tries to brush it off.

"Who says it won't happen now? Tell me and let me be the judge of that."

"I always wanted to be a stay-at-home mom, like my mom was to me. But that dream went out the window with my marriage." She says, staring at her feet.

I feel like I need to tread carefully here. I don't want to scare her, but she has been so hurt that she doesn't want to hope again. I lean forward, tucking my fist under her chin, and then gently turn her face up to me.

"That dream isn't gone. You don't let him take that from you. If you want kids and to be a stay-at-home mom, I'll gladly give that to you, when you're ready. You're going to be an amazing mom, and any guy would be lucky to be along for that ride." I pour my heart out to her and watch her eyes mist over.

"Thank you, Royce," she whispers.

I lean forward and place a chaste kiss on her lips. Short, sweet, and soft.

"Your turn." I urge her on.

"You said you just bought a small ranch, and your family just moved to the area a few months ago, so what exactly is it that you do for a living?"

I smile because it's a basic question, but one that every wife should know.

"Well, I do a lot of woodworking. Maggie helped me set up a website, and I take in custom orders, and I also have my stuff on consignment at a shop in Dallas."

"What kind of stuff?" She asks.

"Well, a little bit of everything. I specialize in custom order dollhouses, but I make birdhouses and small toys, too."

She laughs, and I hold on to the sound. It's just like that first day in the beauty shop. That laugh just calls to me.

"How did you get into custom dollhouses?" She asks.

I chuckle, too. "When Maggie and Ella were younger, money was tight; I knew that more so than Maggie and Ella, being the oldest. One year for her birthday, Maggie wanted this dollhouse she saw at the store, but we couldn't afford it. So, I talked to my dad about me building one. We spent two months on it. We went to the store several times to get things right, and then I customized it with things Maggie loved at the time." I smile at the memory. It was a great time with my dad.

"Maggie loved it, and Ella begged me to make her one, too. So, I did. Their friends loved it, and their parents started asking to buy them. So, it became a good little side hobby with people from church. I was making more than I could on my part-time job, while in school. When Maggie learned websites, she set one up, and we did some research on prices. She posted on social media her story, and it went somewhat viral. I've had a steady stream of requests since. I actually have a waiting list."

Her eyes are wide "Wow! I loved my dollhouse growing up. That's such an awesome job. Do you work at the house?"

"Yeah, I set up the garage as my work area. I guess at some point, I'll have to build a proper workroom on the ranch, so you can get your car in the garage."

"What why?" She asks confused.

"Well, to protect your car, but especially, so you don't have to go out in the rain or snow to get in your car or get in the house."

"What about you?" She asks.

"I'm fine. Like I said, I will always take care of you."

"I'm starting to see that cowboy. Why don't we go to bed? I'm excited to see what you have planned tomorrow."

"Okay, but I'll apologize now because we've got an early morning."

I love how happy she looks going to bed tonight, and I'm up way later than I should be just to commit that smile and laugh to memory.

Chapter 4

Anna Mae

I'm awake, as the first rays of morning start to fill the room. I'm more excited about today than I realized. A day away from the others to figure us out is exactly what I need.

My head has been all over the place with being married. I know I'm not ready to let Royce go, but I'm sure as hell not ready to do the whole vulnerable married thing again. This seems like a nice compromise.

I turn over, and my eyes go right to Royce on the couch. He's been very respectful and caring, and I hope he doesn't change, once we get home to Rock Springs. Though, my heart knows he won't. This is the Royce I've gotten to know over the last year.

Not wanting to get out of bed just yet, I take a pillow from the bed and whip it at Royce. It hits him in the back of the head just enough to wake him up. He stretches and gives me a view of those amazing muscles, which I got a clear view of that first morning.

Then, he looks over at me, and I try to hide the grin on my face and fail.

He jumps up and has me pinned to the bed in no time flat, causing me to squeal.

"Good morning, my wife."

His gruff morning voice is sexy as hell, and I start to reconsider a day in bed over going out. I feel safe and cherished in his arms like this, and I don't want to move.

"In a playful mood, are we?" He asks, nipping at my neck, before standing back up. "All the better, so we can get an early start. Let's get dressed and head down for breakfast."

We get ready and share the bathroom like we have been doing it for years. Never in each other's way and almost in perfect sync, like it was meant to be. Is that possible?

He takes my hand, as we head downstairs, and like every morning, he helps with my plates at the buffet, and as we sit down, I realize I forgot to grab a knife.

"Shoot. I need to go grab a knife. I'll be right back." I say and start to stand when he takes my hand.

"Stay and eat. I'll get it for you." He's up and going back to the buffet, before I can say anything. I stare at him the entire time. This is what every woman dreams of, right? The guy who wants to take care of you. But it can't last. Nothing this good lasts. I will enjoy this ride, while I can.

"Here you go, my sweet girl." He hands me the knife, as he sits back down. I set the knife down and pull him in for a kiss right there in the dining room for anyone who is watching.

"Thank you," I say.

He chuckles. "If I can get a kiss like that every time you forget something, then please forget more things."

Breakfast is fun and easy, as we talk about what everyone else is doing today. I guess my grandma is hitting her hot spots at the casinos again with Jason's parents. Maggie's parents are going with her and Nick on a food tour, and the other couples are hitting a few water parks.

"Why didn't Nick's parents come to Vegas with us?" I ask as the thought pops into my head.

"Nick offered, but his mom wanted to stay and get things going for the wedding. His dad offered to run WJ's for them, so both Nick and Jason could go away for the weekend without shutting the place down." Royce tells me.

WJ's is the bar Jason inherited, and with the help from his wife, Ella, and Nick's award-winning BBQ, they turned it into a family restaurant that now draws people in from as far as Dallas, which is over an hour away.

As we finish up, Royce takes my plates for me, and we head out, and it's then I notice a set of keys in his hand.

"What's that?" I ask.

"Oh, I rented us a car for the day."

"Where are we going?" Many thoughts whirl around in my head.

"Surprise." He winks at me and helps me into an SUV.

"Big car for just two people," I say when he gets in.

"Yes, but Las Vegas is full of people, and this is safer for you than some small car." He says, as he leans over and gives me a chaste kiss on the lips. Once he has the navigation pulled up, and we are on the way, he never lets go of my hand.

It's not long before I see the sign for Hoover Dam, and I start to get excited. I've always wanted to visit the dam.

"Are we going to Hoover Dam?" I ask, not even trying to contain my excitement.

Royce laughs, "Well if we weren't, we would be now with how excited you are. But yes, Hoover Dam was the plan."

I almost bounce in my seat the rest of the way there. When we park, I get my first look at how huge the dam really is.

"You know I have wanted to visit here ever since I saw it in that movie *Vegas Vacation*," I tell him.

"Never seen it." He says as he takes my hand, guiding me towards the visitor center.

"When we get home, our first movie night, we have to watch it. I think you'll love it." I say.

"Deal."

On the tour, we get to go through the tunnels, and as we walk through some of the rock tunnels, there's indeed water leaking down them just like in the movie.

"Don't stick your gum on it," I laugh. Royce doesn't get the joke, but the couple behind us does, and we start talking about the differences between the tour and the movie.

We have some good laughs, and they love that we are just married. They have been married for over fifteen years, and they too got married in Las Vegas and visited the dam on their honeymoon. They're here for their anniversary and doing it all over again.

There's a small cafe where we have lunch, before heading back into Las Vegas.

"Where to next?" I ask.

"Well, I thought we'd go back to the strip and just see where the day takes us, but we do have dinner reservations."

The first place we stop is the Las Vegas Venetian, and Royce gets this twinkle in his eye.

"Come on." He tugs on my hand, and of course, I follow, like I have much of a choice.

"Care for a gondola ride, my wife?" He says, as we round the corner and see the famous gondolas that replicate the ones in Venice, Italy.

"Yes!" I squeal. Royce is nailing it today, he knows me so well. As we head inside, there are bridges we go under, and the ceiling is painted and lit up like the sky, and it's all so romantic.

We get on the gondola, and the boat driver starts singing some romantic Italian song, as I snuggle into Royce, and he kisses the top of my head.

I sigh at how perfect of a moment this.

"Everything okay, sweet girl?" He asks.

"Yes, this is perfect here with you like this," I whisper.

He pulls out his phone, and we take a few photos and just enjoy the time in each other's arms.

After our ride, we walk through some of the shops and then head back out to the strip just in time to see the Mirage's Volcano erupt across the street.

"I almost think you planned that." I joke with him.

"I'm not even that good." He laughs and slings his arm over my shoulders, as we keep walking.

As we pass by Cesar's, there are signs for Gordon Ramsey's Hell's Kitchen Restaurant.

"Oh, I love that show! Are we eating at Hell's Kitchen?" I ask.

"Nope, I think I did even better than that." He says with a smile on his face.

As we reach the Bellagio, we head into their restaurant. Once we follow the hostess to our seats, I see where we are eating and gasp. The walls are all glass, and we are right next to the fountain. When the shows start, we will be right in the action.

"Oh, Royce, this is amazing!" I gush.

Royce, as always, pulls out my chair and gets me settled, before he sits down.

"So, tell me about this house of yours," I ask to get him talking.

"Well, you know it's fifty acres, four bedrooms, and two bathrooms. It needs a bit of work and a woman's touch for sure. There's a barn, so I was thinking of boarding some horses. There's plenty of room for a garden near the house, and we can keep some livestock on the rest of the land, if not to sell them to keep our fridge full." The waitress brings our drinks, and we order before he continues.

"I set up a workshop in the garage, but there are several outbuildings, so I'll move that there. If you want to set up one of the rooms for a hobby or side business, you're more than welcome, too."

"And you just got in the consignment place in Dallas. What do you sell there?"

"I do a lot of smaller items. Things Texas or cowboy-related, small toys, or some fancy shelves. I make that stuff between dollhouse orders, and then go up once a month to give them what I have. You should come with me when I go next time."

"I'd like that. I want to see your work."

"So, Maggie said you just won some award?" He asks.

"Oh, yes. In Dallas, they do hair expos and hair shows to show off what you can do. Jill and I go to get the beauty shop name out there. I won an award for wedding hairstyles. Megan's excited because she's booked two large wedding parties from it. I guess, the B&B in town has an event barn, and barn weddings are all the rage right now."

The conversation flows and is so easy, as we finish dinner and get to see the water show twice, before making our way back to our room. The more we talk about life back in Rock Springs, the more I see a life with him there.

It's scary to let myself want it because I really do want it. I just hope this all works out in the end, even though, I don't see how. Friends with benefits is about all I can give, and I hope it's enough. It seems to be right now. It all feels so natural walking down the sidewalk arm in arm, like any other couple.

As we are walking into the lobby, we run into Mac and Sarah.

"Hey, you guys enjoy your honeymoon?" Mac asks with a huge knowing smile on his face.

"We had a great day. We did Hoover Dam, had a gondola ride, walked The Strip, and had dinner next to the water fountain show. It's been incredible." I gush.

"Oh, that all sounds so romantic!" Sarah says as Mac wraps his arm around her waist.

"Hey, we had a romantic day by the pool." Mac pouts.

"Yes, until you threw a towel over me because you said too many guys were looking at me!" Sarah smacks his chest, pretending to be upset, but the smile on her face tells a different story.

"They were, and I didn't like it," Mac says, and we all laugh.

"Can't say I blame you," Royce says and squeezes my hand. I can see Royce doing the same thing with me, and I smile. I have always loved how the guys in Megan's family are with their girls, and to have a guy that does that for me now, is exciting.

We say our goodbyes, promising to meet up for breakfast before we head to the airport tomorrow.

Chapter 5

Anna Mae

When I open my eyes, my head is buzzing a lot, like it was the morning I woke up married. Except this time, it's not from the alcohol, it's from traveling home.

Once we got into Dallas, we still had over an hour's drive back to Rock Springs. Then, Royce drove my grandma home and insisted on bringing over a load of my stuff in his truck. I don't have much, just my clothes and some boxes, so we spent an hour and packed up my room. This weekend we will go back and get my stuff that's being stored in my grandma's garage.

So, by the time we got home, unloaded my stuff, and he gave me a house tour, it was almost three a.m.

I get up and go in search of Royce. I hate to admit even to myself that I didn't like him sleeping at the other end of the house. Even though we haven't been sharing a bed, I got used to him being in the same room as me at night. I walk into the kitchen and get a good look at the time, and it's seven a.m.

The kitchen is set up like a farmhouse kitchen with a large farmhouse sink, painted wood cabinets, and butcher block countertops. It could use a few modern touches and a coat of paint, but all in all, it's cozy.

On the counter is a plate with a few blueberry muffins, and a note from Royce.

Wife,

Not sure what you eat for breakfast, but Ella made these blueberry muffins, and they are some of my favorites. Orange juice is in the fridge and fresh coffee is on the counter. Unpack your stuff and make yourself at home. I'm out in my workshop if you need me.

Love,

Royce

I sit at the kitchen table, eating the muffins and having some coffee. I need to remember to thank Ella for the muffins because they are really good. After I finish, I head back to my room to take a shower and get dressed. Then, I unpack my boxes.

I put away my clothes and put a few photos of my grandma and me and some of my parents and brother around the room. After I unpack my suitcase from Las Vegas, I go on the hunt for the laundry room to wash my dirty clothes. I find it near the kitchen and notice that I don't even have half a load, and then a thought hits me.

I hesitantly make my way to Royce's room and find his dirty clothes in the hamper in his bathroom. Taking them, I add mine and run a load. It just makes sense, I tell myself. Nothing more to it, than saving water and energy.

Once done, I head out to find Royce because I want to watch him work. The garage is connected to the laundry room, so I open the door and peek out.

His back is to me, and he's sanding down the framework of a dollhouse. Even with just the bare bones in place, I can tell it's going to be beautiful.

When the door closes behind me, he stops and turns towards me with a huge smile, lighting up his face.

"Good morning, beautiful." He says and walks over to place a kiss on my cheek. "Did you eat breakfast?"

"Yes, those muffins were delicious," I tell him.

"Did you unpack?"

"Yep, I even started a load of laundry. I hope you don't mind, but I tossed some of your stuff in with mine. I didn't want to run only half a load."

"I don't mind at all. Thank you. But I want you to know, I don't expect you to take care of me. That's not why I want you here."

"I know. We'll get into a routine, but it will take time. So, show me what you're working on." I nod towards the dollhouse in hopes of changing the subject.

We spend the next few hours talking about the dollhouse, as I watch him work. We get ready to take a break for lunch when he wraps his arms around my waist and pulls me into him. I wrap my arms around his neck like it's the most natural thing to do.

"I enjoy having you in my space like this," he says and kisses me.

He goes for a soft, quick kiss, but I pull him back in for more. I can tell I caught him off guard, but he hides it quickly, as he takes control of the kiss and deepens it. For someone who doesn't have much experience in this department, he sure knows how to set my whole body on fire.

When he pulls back, he rests his forehead on mine and whispers, "I really, really like having you in my space."

I laugh and kiss the tip of his nose. "Come on, cowboy. Give me the grand tour, and then I'll make you lunch."

"Okay, let's start outside." He leads me onto the back porch, and it's the porch I have always pictured. Large enough for kids to play on it, while the adults gather at the back. There's a fire pit with chairs on one side and chairs with a grill on the other.

I guess I stand for a long time in one spot looking around because Royce comes up and wraps his arm around my waist.

"We can change anything you want." He says in my ear.

"Oh, Royce, I love this back porch. I was just picturing sitting out here after dinner, or even having breakfast out here."

"It's one of my favorite spots, too."

I turn to face him, and there's a slight smile on his lips.

"Yet, you were going to let me change it?" I ask. If he loved this spot so much, why would he want me to change it?

He shrugs his shoulder. "I come out here for the view of the land; the quiet. I don't care what it looks like, and if changing it makes you happy, then that's all that matters."

I hug him then, burying my face into his chest, so he doesn't see my eyes mist over. Part of me was wondering if he was only being so sweet in Vegas to get me to move in, but my heart knows this is just Royce, and he's always been this way.

"Okay, cowboy, show me the land," I say, once my emotions are in check.

He spends an hour showing me the barn and a few of the outbuildings and giving me a ride on the gator around the property. As we head back inside, he pulls me over to the side of the house, where there's a small garden.

"Ella started a garden here, and she picked the spot best for it. I know the basics, but she's the one who's good at it. We can grow anything you like."

"Well, Ella will have to come out and teach me a thing or two, because I've never tended a garden before. Never lived on this much land either."

I take a deep breath of the country air, and I know in my bones I'm going to love it out here. It's quiet and peaceful, and your neighbors aren't right on top of you, knowing every move you make. It hasn't even been twenty-four hours, and this place already feels like home.

"Come on, let's take a look inside, and you can start getting some decorating ideas." He says, and we head inside.

The house looks much different in the light of day, much brighter and homier.

The living room is done in creams and blues that pair nicely with the large, stone fireplace, which he has family photos everywhere on the mantel.

"Ella and Sarah did this room, and our... my... bedroom for me, when I moved in, but we can redo them however you want."

I caught that he called his room our room, even if I'm not staying there. I wonder if he bought this place with me in mind, or if he pictured me in this space with him when he first saw it.

I decide not to harp on the issue right now.

"What do you use the other rooms for?" I nod down the hallway, where my room is.

"I had the one you're using set up as a guest room, but it's all yours, so do what you will with it. The one across the hall I set up as an office. I can get you a desk in here too, so you can use it if you want." He says as he opens the door to the room across from mine.

"I don't need a desk." I wave him off.

"Well, I'll get you one anyway. We can get you a computer set up, so you can do research on new hairstyles and local competitions. I was thinking I can talk to Megan and see about having her help us get a chair that we can set at the end of the hall. You could use it to try new hairstyles or practice for the competitions. I know Jason's sisters would be more than happy to let you."

"Royce..." I don't even know what to say to that.

"Just think about it, but you can do whatever you want with that room. There are just a few boxes in it." He opens the door and shows me. While it's a bit smaller than mine, it would make a great workspace.

"This bathroom is all yours, though the master bathroom, is much nicer, so you're free to use it whenever you want."

"Will you show me?" I ask. I only got a small peek, when I got his clothes earlier because I was uninvited and felt like I was an intruder in his space.

He nods and takes my hand, leading me to the other side of the house. His bedroom is decorated in the same creams as the living room, but with woodsy green accents, instead of blue. It's very light, bright, and relaxing. There are several photos of different sizes above the bed of nature, trees, and open fields.

"This room feels like you," I say more to myself than to him. "Who took these photos?"

He chuckles. "Ella knows me so well that she decorated my room for me back in Tennessee, too. She and Maggie loved to decorate the house, and my parents let them. The photos are Maggie's, and all of them were taken on this property."

His love for his sisters shows, and I have to admit it makes me miss my brother.

"My brother was protective, but he wouldn't have let me touch his room like that."

I step closer to look at the photos. One long horizontal picture looks up a tree with light, peeking through the top. Another is of a wide pasture with a house in the distance. Looking closer, I see it's the house we are in.

"The bathroom is just through there." He points to a door, and this time I take a look around the bathroom. There's a large clawfoot tub that could easily fit two people and a walk-in shower with a rainfall showerhead.

"Wow," I whisper.

"So, move your stuff in here and use this one. I don't mind."

"I'll take you up on that, especially for that tub."

We head back to the kitchen, and I start on lunch. Royce says he's going to wash up. I'm lost in the thought of squeezing in a bath in that amazing tub when my phone rings.

I pull it out and freeze. Liam, my ex, is calling. I silence the phone, send him to voicemail, and put it away. I'm not ready to talk to him. Hell, I don't ever want to talk to him again. Maybe, he will leave me a voice mail, and I can have my grandma listen to it and tell me if it's important. Cowards way out, I know.

As I make us some sandwiches, my mind drifts to the day after Liam and I were first married. We honeymooned in Key West, Florida, but he never wanted to leave the bedroom, so I didn't see much of the place. It felt like a waste. Such a different honeymoon than with Royce, who packed a full day of stuff he knew I'd love.

Then, when we got home, Liam expected me to unpack his clothes and do the laundry. I had moved into his condo, and he didn't want me changing anything up without talking to him. He couldn't wait to rush back to work and made sure that I knew he expected me to have dinner on the table. Oh, and by the way, I could find my way around the neighborhood, right?

Such night and day from Royce. I'm pulled from my thoughts, as I finish the sandwiches, and I hear the dryer start. Royce comes out of the laundry room, and I stop in my tracks.

"Did you switch the clothes over?" I ask, more stunned than anything.

"Yeah, why? Did you have something that can't go in the dryer?" He turns to stop the dryer.

"No, it's just... Thank you. I'm not used to someone else helping around the house that isn't my grandma."

Royce's face goes soft. "I told you, you aren't here to take care of me. It's my job to take care of you. After lunch, why don't you relax? You go back to work tomorrow, so enjoy the rest of the day off. Take a bath or a nap."

We finish lunch, and he talks about the dollhouse he's working on and a few smaller items he has to go up to the consignment store in a few weeks.

After lunch, he kisses me on the cheek and then heads out to his workshop. I clean up the lunch dishes and go into the living room, thinking I will watch some TV, but I stop dead in my tracks. My photos from my room have been mixed in with his all over the room.

Yeah, he's nothing like Liam, and maybe, it's about time I give him a real chance.

Chapter 6

Anna Mae

Today is the first of our weekly dates. I asked to go horseback riding, so I could see more of the land and get to know it better. I figure I'm living out here, so it can't hurt to know my way around it.

So, Royce planned a picnic at one of his favorite spots. I'm looking around the barn, as we are getting ready to head out.

"You only have the two horses?" I ask.

"Only need two. One for you, and one for me," he nods to the one I'm saddling up. "I got her with you in mind, hoping I'd be able to convince you to go riding with me."

"What's her name?"

"Well, she was a rescue, so she doesn't have one. It's up to you to give her a name."

"Hmm, she looks like nice warm caramel, so I'll call her Caramel," I say, and when I do, she neighs and nods her head. "I think she likes it."

He laughs, "Looks like she does." He leans in to pet her. "You take care of my wife, Caramel, and I'll have extra treats for you when we're done." The horse nods again like she can understand, and he gives her a kiss on her nose.

Then, he turns to me and helps me up into the saddle. I watch him mount his horse, whose name is Thunder. There's something about a cowboy on a horse that has my body begging to go for a ride, too.

The ride to the picnic spot isn't that far, and on the way, we talk about our week. Royce tells me about the progress he's making on the dollhouse, which is almost done. It's amazing to me the progress he has made each day, while I'm at work.

I tell him about some of the gossip at the salon, which mostly centers on a few new guys around town. Ranchers are getting tense from the illegal rodeo running nearby and are bringing on extra hands to stand guard. Last we heard, there are now eight missing horses from the Rock Springs area. One of them was found dead in a ditch three counties over, and tensions have been high ever since.

We've been letting them talk and keeping an ear to the ground for the sheriff, as Megan asked, but we also don't let them stay on the topic too long and try to steer them to more cheerful gossip, which always backfires to them wanting to know more about my Vegas wedding. I've talked more about that weekend than the rest of my life combined.

When we reach a small clearing at the back of the property, Royce stops and just stares.

"This is what sold me on the land. It's the perfect picnic spot. I can imagine kids playing, getting my sisters and their kids together, and having family days out here. It's easy to get a truck in too, going along the north edge of the property."

He looks lost in thought, as his face softens, and his brown eyes sparkle of summer days with kids running around, and for a brief second, I can see it too, and I want it more than anything. But then, reality comes crashing back.

I won't have that.

So, I plaster on a big smile, get down from my horse, and then tie him to a nearby tree. When I turn around, Royce has done the same and is unloading the picnic supplies. I grab the blanket from him, and we head to the center of the clearing, where the sun is shining and will offer just enough warmth to chase away the last of the spring chill.

"Ella tells me that Abby is coming back into town this summer. Did you meet her, when she was here over Christmas break?" Royce asks.

"Briefly. She's studying to become a midwife, right?"

"Yeah, Ella says she'll work with a doctor nearby to be at a few births over the summer, while she's visiting. With Megan being due in two months, she's hoping to go late, so Abby will be here like she was for Riley."

I laugh, "Honestly, I'm surprised there haven't been any more baby announcements from that family. They'll be overrun with kids soon enough." I smile and think of all five couples having babies soon. "It's a good thing their ranch is the second biggest in Texas. For sure, they'll need the space"

The more we chat, the more I realize how easy it is to talk to Royce. He listens, asks questions, and pays attention, even to the smallest things. It's such a night and day difference compared to Liam, who didn't want to hear about it if it didn't affect him. He'd rush through a meal to get up and get work done. Where Royce is relaxed, while slowly eating.

"Would you like to go for a walk?" Royce asks as we finish lunch.

"Sure." He helps me stand and takes my hand, as we walk to the other end of the tree line.

"So, how did I do on our first official date?" He asks as we reach the fence at the end of his property.

"I had a great time. I love how peaceful it is out here, and how easy you are to talk to. Plus, any date that starts with me getting my own horse is a win in my book."

Royce throws his head back in an unfiltered laugh.

"I like you like this," I say without thinking.

The smile stays on his face, as his eyes scan over my face.

"Like how?" He asks.

"Like this, stress-free and laughing. You seem in your element out here."

"It's because I am." He takes my hand again, as we turn and walk back towards the clearing.

"So, next date, I was thinking we head into town and catch the live band that will be at WJ's next week?"

"I'd love that. Megan's been raving about this new taco dish Nick just added to the menu, and I want to try it."

"Perfect. I can't wait to dance with you, since we didn't get to dance at our wedding. Well, not that I know of anyway." He chuckles.

"I can't wait to dance with you, too," I admit.

We just make it to the clearing, when Royce's phone goes off.

"It's Ella." He says, before answering.

"Hey. Wait, let me put you on speaker." He pulls the phone away and presses a few buttons.

"Okay, Anna Mae is here, so start over."

"Lilly just called. A third horse was just found tied to the back of their barn. Hunter, Sage, and Colt are on their way there now to help out. It's the same pattern. The horse is so thin you can see every bone, and it's scared and beaten so bad. The only way it's still standing is it has to be drugged, like the others."

"And there are no leads?" Royce asks.

"Well, this time there are tire tracks and some footprints, so the cops are there and won't let anyone touch the horse until they make sure there's no other evidence. It's not much to go on, but it's more than the last two times. Since this is the second horse left on their property, Lilly said the state police are going to put cameras up, and they have some on the church too, where the last horse was left."

"Any others been stolen in the area lately?" Royce asks.

"No, but someone did show up with a state police officer to claim Black Diamond, the first horse. He's all better, and Lilly and Sage have been working with him. The man thought he could walk in with the paperwork and walk out with the horse. Mike said they wouldn't let him go until he paid the bill, which included the vet's services, boarding, and training. When the guy saw the bill, he flipped. The officer said they had every legal right, so he signed the horse over to Lilly and Mike on the spot." Ella says.

"Wow, at least they have papers on one, but this is something that could happen to all of them," Royce says, lost in thought.

"Oh, it gets better," Ella continues. "The police then found out he had already claimed insurance money on the horse. When the police updated the police report, the insurance company was notified, and now they are demanding payment back since he gave the horse to Mike and Lilly and suffered none of the costs."

I can't help it, I bust out laughing. "Karma strikes again," I say, causing Ella to giggle.

"Yep, in the best possible way." She agrees.

"Okay, keep us updated, and please, stay safe. Call me if you need me, no matter what time." Royce says.

"Okay, you stay safe too big brother. I love you, and I love you too, sister-in-law of mine." Ella says.

"Love you, Ella bug," Royce says, as we finish our goodbyes.

As we walk up to the horses, I just can't wrap my head around the situation.

"How can someone be so cruel to one of these amazing creatures?" I ask as I pet the top of Carmel's head, and she brushes her head against mine.

"Some people are just wired differently. They are driven by money and will do anything to get it, no matter the cost. They think money will solve any problem when in reality, it just creates more problems for them." Royce says.

He helps me back on my horse, before securing the rest of our stuff and climbing up on Thunder. His visible muscles, even through his jacket, catch my eye. He turns and catches me watching him, as my cheeks heat at the embarrassment of being caught.

Royce walks his horse right up beside mine.

"You can watch any time, my wife. I'm all yours, and I rather like you checking me out." He says in a gritty voice that washes over me and turns me on with each word.

Taking a different way back to the house, he shows me some of the berry bushes that will be ready for picking in a few weeks. I start planning some jams to make, and maybe, even some pies. I could invite Ella over to show me how to make those amazing muffins she made for us.

We take the horses back to the barn and brush them down. I find this part relaxing and bonding time with the horse. We both work in silence, only occasionally talking to our horses. I take longer than he does, and he waits to walk me inside.

We pause at the back door, and he turns to look at me.

"I had a really good time today." He says as he runs his eyes over me in the way that I'm quickly coming to love. It's like he's studying me to learn my reaction and make sure nothing is out of place.

"I did, too. Maybe, we can make it a regular thing outside for our weekly dates? It was fun, and it might be a good way to relax on the weekend." I ask a bit hesitantly.

"Anything you want, sweet girl." He murmurs, as he starts to close the distance between us. The second his eyes land on my lips, I know he's going to kiss me, and I know I want him too more than I should.

When his lips touch mine, it sets my whole body on fire. I can't get enough of him, as I wrap my arms around his waist, pulling him closer. His hands, on either side of my head, gently moves my face, so he can get a better angle. His tongue tangles with mine in slow, lazy strokes, before he nibbles on my bottom lip, and then pulls away, resting his forehead on mine.

We both take a moment to catch our breaths.

"I love you, my wife." He whispers against my lips, before giving me another chaste kiss.

I freeze then because I don't know what to say. Thank you seems inadequate, but not saying anything seems even worse. I don't want to hurt him, but love just isn't in the cards for me anymore.

He smiles and gently rubs his nose against mine.

"It's okay. You say it when you're ready, because I do plan to make you fall in love with me, and I'm a very patient guy." He kisses the tip of my nose, before opening the door for me.

I retreat to my room to process everything that just happened. I think I need a girl's night because it's all becoming too much.

Chapter 7

Anna Mae

I'm standing in the beauty shop today, and I'm having a hard time paying attention to the girls, as they chat about the latest gossip. I didn't expect to like living with Royce as much as I do. He's sweet and thoughtful, and always doing things for me. Yesterday, I came home, and he had all the laundry done, folded, and put away.

Every day when I work, I come home to him making dinner. On the days I have off, we cook dinner together. He always has time for me, and he enjoys me in his space when he's working, and I love watching him work.

We have settled into a great routine of having breakfast and coffee together in the morning, having dinner together, and watching TV in the evenings. Last night, I fell asleep during the movie, and I woke up to him carrying me to my bed and tucking me in.

He's making it very hard to keep my walls up and protect my heart. The worst part is he isn't trying to break down my defenses. He's just being himself, and that makes it even easier for him to break through them.

"What do you think, Anna Mae?" Megan says to me, pulling me from my mental fog.

"Sorry, what was the question?" I ask.

Megan shoots me a knowing smile. "I asked what you think about Kelli and that new ranch hand. Rumor is they're sleeping together."

I shrug my shoulders. "Wouldn't surprise me. Kelli will sleep with anything with a pulse, and most ranch hands wouldn't turn it down. If he's new, he doesn't know her history, so it's not impossible."

Kelli isn't well liked with the ladies of the salon. She won't even come in to get her hair done, since Megan owns the place. She was a key point of tension between Sage and Colt, when they were having some problems, and even became pretty vicious trying to break them up at the end. But they both saw her for the snake she is, and so did the rest of the town after that.

"What I want to know is what you all think of this new guy. I get the creeps every time he's around, and I wouldn't be surprised if he has something to do with this illegal rodeo around here. Though, I can't prove it." I say.

The girls agree. "There's just something not right around him," Jill says. "And it's not just because he's hooking up with Kelli."

"Jason feels the same way. He's talked to him a few times at WJ's, and he's in every weekend. Last weekend, Jason was tending the bar, because his bartender was sick, and the guy treated everyone around him like crap. He didn't see who he left with, but Kelli left about the same time, too." Megan confirms.

The next few hours are pretty much the same things being repeated with every batch of new clients that come in. As the day winds down, Megan sits and puts her feet up on the couch in the waiting area. She's seven months pregnant, and as much as her husband wants her to stay home, she won't. She loves the people here too much, she says.

"So, we are still on for girl's night, right Anna Mae? Ella has been cooking up a storm, and even promised to have more muffins for you," Megan says.

I didn't know who else to call for girl's night, so when I mentioned it to Ella, she called her sisters-in-law up. I guess, girl's night is a monthly thing with them, and they were more than happy to include me because they think of Ella's brother as family, and now, me by extension.

Royce about kicked me out of the house this morning, saying to enjoy myself, and that his sisters Ella and Maggie were looking forward to some girl time. I guess, even Lilly is coming over.

I wanted to bring something too, so I made my grandma's fudge brownies last night. I made two batches, one for Royce and me, and one for me to take tonight. Though, I had to hide them in Megan's office, since we are heading there right after work.

Royce even tried to encourage me to pack a bag in case I wanted to drink, so I could stay the night, but I didn't. I decided not to drink because as much as I don't want to admit it to him, I want to come home to him tonight, even if it's late, and he's already asleep. I enjoy our routines.

"I'll be there. I need some girl time, and it's been a whirlwind since Vegas." I say.

"No details!" Megan shouts. "I promised the girls not to let you talk, until we all got there, so they don't miss anything."

I can't help but laugh, I didn't know how much I missed having friends until I started working here with Megan, and even more now, since Royce and I have been married.

During the drive to the ranch, I debate what all I will tell them. I know I can trust these ladies and decide to go for broke. I need to figure out what to do.

Megan and I are the last ones there, and they have food spread out all over the kitchen.

"I brought my grandma's brownies," I say, and a cheer goes up across the room.

"I'll take these," Sage says and sets them out for everyone.

"Okay, ladies. Fill your plates and grab a comfy spot in the living room. Drinks are out there, both alcoholic and non-alcoholic, and we'll start the night, once we all have food. I expect to see mountains on those plates! Girl's night is a no diets allowed night, so don't be stingy!" Riley says.

"Where's the baby?" I ask her.

"With her dad. He says I hog her too much, so he was taking her for some daddy time." She rolls her eyes at me.

Once we have our plates filled with tacos, fried chicken, sides, bread, and desserts, we all pile into the living room.

I grab a tea, as Sarah stops me. "Try the margaritas. They're amazing."

"No, thank you. I haven't had alcohol, since the night I woke up married. I doubt I'll ever drink again." I try to laugh it off, but I'm completely serious. This time marriage, next time, who knows.

The girls laugh and mostly agree with me, as I sit down.

"Okay, who's up first?" Riley asks.

"Me! I'm dying and don't want to be pregnant anymore!" Megan says dramatically.

"Well, I'll be in your shoes soon," Ella says with a huge grin on her face.

"What!" We all yell at the same time.

"We're due in November, and I'm about eight weeks give or take. We have to go to the doctor next week."

We all take turns hugging her. When it's my turn, I hug her extra tight. She's after all my sister-in-law. "Does Royce know?"

"No, but you can tell him, and then let him know I'll talk to him tomorrow." She says.

"You and Jason need to come over for dinner to celebrate," I say.

"Any time!" Ella agrees as we all start eating again.

I look up, and Megan is giving me the tell them look with her stern face, and her eyes darting to the girls.

"Well, I guess the real reason we're here is me," I start.

"Oh, good cause it was killing me!" Sage says, causing laughter around the room.

"I woke up married, and I don't remember a thing. I'm pretty sure we had sex because we woke up naked, but I didn't feel like we had sex, ya know? Now, I'm living with him, and he's sweet and kind. I have trust issues and never wanted to get married again. I'm afraid I'm going to hurt him, so I need HELP!" I suck in a deep breath at the end of my rant, and every woman in the room is just looking at me.

Sage chugs a bit of her margarita, as do Lilly and Sarah.

"Okay, one thing at a time. I say we start with the trust issues. We know the basics. Your ex cheated on you and knocked up his secretary." Riley says.

"Yep, and then kicked me to the curb so fast that if it wasn't for my grandma and Megan, I don't know where I'd be."

Megan blows me a kiss from where she's laying on the couch with her feet up over Sarah and Riley's laps.

"Well, it's been over a year. I know it's hard to trust. Believe me, I know. But it can happen slowly, and it doesn't have to be this huge, big leap all at once." Sage says.

"Royce has a kind heart, and he's very understanding. You just have to talk to him and be honest with him." Maggie says.

"I have been. He wants to make this work and has done just about everything he can to make that happen. I have my own room, he cooks me dinner the nights I work, and he asked for weekly date nights, to set aside time for each other once a week. Then, there are little things like learning my favorite foods or my favorite items. He noticed my shampoo was running low and picked some up for me the other day. He's night and day from Liam, and I know that in my head, but my heart isn't listening."

"The heart is funny. You can know someone is your soul mate and still run scared. Look at me. I met Colt, when I was six, and knew I was in love with him when I was in high school. He did everything right, and then one night said one sentence that gave me flashbacks to my sperm donor, so I freaked. I ran, and it was years before we got our second chance." Sage says. "Just don't run and let him help you through it."

"You really have your own room?" Sarah asks. "How do you do it? Royce is hot. I mean, not as hot as Mac, but sorry Ella and Maggie, he is. I wouldn't be able to keep my hands off him." Sarah fans herself.

"Trust me, my body wants him, so that's not the issue. Sex just means so much to him, whereas for me, it's more of a release and just casual. Plug your ears, Ella and Maggie." I say, warning them.

"Please, unless you are going to show a picture of his dick, there isn't anything we don't know," Ella says, as she puts more food in her mouth.

I think everyone's jaw drops at that one, and Maggie busts out laughing.

"I like pregnant, sassy Ella. Please, keep her around after the baby is born," Maggie says.

"Anyway, he's a virgin or was before our wedding night. Neither of us remembers that night, so I guess in a way he technically still is. Where I could have casual sex and be fine, it would be so much more to him, and every one of you know that."

"It would be because it's an intimate and personal thing. He loves you, Anna Mae, and not a single person with eyes can doubt that." Maggie says softly, rubbing my arm.

"I know, and he tells me that, but I freeze every time he does, and I know I'm hurting him, but I just can't say it back," I say.

"How do you feel about him?" Maggie asks.

I stop and think about it. How do I feel about him?

"If I met him before Liam, I know I could fall for him. But now? I don't think I'm capable of falling for anyone or to open myself up like that again. I'm attracted to him, and my body craves him. I love being around him and snuggling up to him and feeling safe. He's really easy to talk to, and he makes me laugh so easily. I guess, if I were to fall in love with anyone again, it would be him." I drop my eyes to my plate at my confession, and the room is quiet before Lilly speaks.

"Then give it time. Time heals all wounds, and you might learn to trust again." Lilly says, and everyone agrees.

I start to believe them before reality comes crashing in. My phone rings, and again, it's Liam. I send him to voice mail.

"And then, the universe says don't listen to them. That was Liam, and it's the second time he's called me in a week." I say.

"What does he want?" Megan asks.

"I don't know. I don't want to talk to him, so I send it to voice mail, but he doesn't leave a message."

"You should tell Royce. Don't keep it from him." Sage says. I nod and agree, because I know I should.

We all finish eating and chat a bit more before we call it a night. On the way home, I hope Royce is up and waiting for me. Normally, he's in bed by now, and I wouldn't be surprised if he's asleep.

As I turn into the driveway, the living room light is on, and I start to hope that maybe he did stay up.

Stepping onto the front porch, I know I'm not quite ready to tell him about Liam calling yet. I know I need to soon, but not tonight. When I open the door, Royce looks over at me, and his whole face lights up.

"Did you have a good time?" He asks as I take my boots off.

"Yeah. You know you could have gone to bed, right?" I tell him.

"I wanted to make sure you got home okay." He says as I sit on the couch next to him. He wraps his arms around me, while I lean my back against him and cuddle up.

"Well, Ella will be calling you tomorrow. She's pregnant." I say.

"Really? Oh, man, my first niece or nephew. I can't wait. We're going to be the best aunt and uncle. We can spoil him or her, and then send them back to mom and dad." He goes on about some of the things he can't wait to do with the baby, but all I hear is him saying we will be the best aunt and uncle.

This baby will be my niece or nephew because we are married. He doesn't know it, but being part of his family, is a huge blessing I never thought I'd get. I'm not close to my parents. They just aren't that kind of people. Though they were good parents and are good people, we never hit that being friends stage Royce seems to have with family. His family that I now get to be a part of.

Seeing him so excited about the new baby on the way, is a huge turn on, and I start to think about adding sex to our relationship, or maybe, we can just fool around a bit. Then, I realize I can't do that to him. When we take that step, I have to be able to give him more.

"Any other good news happen tonight?" He asks.

"Not really. Megan is done being pregnant. Sage and Lilly talked a bit about the new horse, and they tried to bribe my grandma's brownie recipe out of me. All in all, it was fun. I'm glad they asked me to join."

"Maybe, you, Ella, and Maggie can get together and decorate this place. It needs your touch." He says.

"Maybe," I say, knowing I won't. "Oh, we should have Jason and Ella over for dinner to celebrate. Maybe, have Maggie, Nick, and your parents, too."

"I'll make it happen. Now, let's get you to bed. You have had a long day." He says, walking me to my room, before kissing my cheek. I watch him go to his room and almost follow after him, but I stop myself and lock myself in my room.

I don't know how much longer I can hold out.

Chapter 8

Royce

Today, I'm heading to Dallas to take some of my things up to the consignment store. Anna Mae wanted to come with me, but they had called and said they sold the last item and didn't want to leave the shelves bare. If I didn't fill them, someone else would. So, I plan to make a few new things this week, and we can make a special trip up together.

I think a day in Dallas would make a great weekly date. There's so much to do, and I wonder what Anna Mae did when she lived here.

Just like that, it's like a bucket of cold water being thrown on me. Anna Mae used to live here with *him*. Anything she's wanted to do, she probably already did with *him*.

She doesn't talk about her ex-husband. I know the basics, but I hope maybe one day soon she will sit down and talk to me. I wonder if she's comparing me to him, or how he treated her, even before all the cheating?

How long were they married? Long enough for her to go to school to get her cosmetology license and work in a big salon for a bit.

Then, something starts clicking into place, like puzzle pieces finally fitting. He's the reason she's holding back, I know that. I kept telling myself to show her me and how different I am from him. But maybe, I need to also be working to help her forget about him, so it's not right at the front of everything she does. Maybe then, she can open her heart to me, even just a little.

As I hit the Dallas traffic, my new plan starts to sink in, as my smile returns. I left earlier than I normally would, so I could be back by the time Anna Mae gets off work. That means I'm hitting the tail end of rush hour traffic, coming into the city.

As I'm bringing in the box to the shop, the store owner's daughter rushes up to help me. Her name is Tara, and she has always seemed just a little too nice, but I never paid it much attention. Today, when she tries to help with the box and her arm brushes mine, it makes my skin crawl.

"Royce! I'm so glad you have more stuff for us. It seems to be selling so well." Tara says in such a bubbly voice. "What do you have for us this time?"

We set the boxes down and start to price and label the items to go on the shelf.

"I brought some more of those wood animal puzzles. I left them unpainted again, so the kids can paint them, too. Last time I was here, you had some paint sets, so maybe move them near the shelf, where these are?" I suggest.

"Oh, that's such a good idea! I'll tell my dad when he gets in later today." She says.

It takes a half an hour to price and label everything, and she gushes over every last item.

"Oh, I love this unicorn pull toy! Unicorns are really in right now, so are mermaids." She gushes.

"What do you think of maybe some decor signs for next time? My sister has been asking me to make some for her place, so it wouldn't be hard to make a few extra." I ask.

"I think it's a great idea. The farmhouse rustic style is very popular." She says.

"That's what my sister said, too."

Then, she comes from behind the counter and does something I don't expect. She attaches herself to my arm, almost like we are walking down the aisle of a wedding together.

"With summer coming up, all things red, white, and blue will sell well. Then looking into fall, all things pumpkin. You can do so much with fall decor!"

I pull my arm free from hers and start arranging the items on the shelves. She has never been this handsy when I visit. Then again, her dad is always here, when I come, too.

She doesn't seem to take the hint when she runs a hand up my back. "You know we should go have lunch and talk about the upcoming trends. Maybe, get some good ideas for new stuff."

This is where I know I have to end it. I take a large step away from her touch and try not to shiver, and it's not the kind of shiver Anna Mae's touch gives me. It's more of a creeped out shiver. The first thing I'm going to do when I get home is shower and scrub my back and my arm.

"I don't think my wife would appreciate me having lunch with another woman, who is so blatantly hanging all over me and not taking the subtle hints to stop," I say my voice cold. No emotion, nothing to give her to latch on, too.

Her eyes go wide for a brief moment before she starts laughing. "Oh, good one, Royce. You aren't married!" She says like I just said the funniest joke in the world.

I hold up my left hand and say nothing. She stops laughing, as her eyes go wide again, and her face pales a bit, as her eyes lock on the ring.

It's then I realize I'm still wearing the cheap ring from the Elvis wedding chapel, and so is Anna Mae. I don't like the thought of some guy flirting with her like this, and her not having a proper ring to show them. Of course, the guys who get their hair cut at the shop where she works are Megan's husband, Hunter, and his dad. And now, only me and my dad, if I have anything to say about it.

"When?" She says in a quiet voice.

I let my hand fall back to my side. "A few weeks ago. Small ceremony, only family." I say. I'm not going to mention Las Vegas. She doesn't need to know it wasn't a huge, planned out, done up affair.

"I didn't know you were seeing anyone." She says, trying to save face.

"Why would you? This isn't a personal relationship. It's business. One I normally handle with your dad and prefer to continue to deal with your dad. Now, if you will get my check for me, I want to make it home, before my wife does."

I grab the boxes I carried everything in with and wait for her, as she heads behind the counter and hands me an envelope with my check from the last round of consignments.

I go back out to my truck, and as soon as the door closes, some of the tension falls away, but not all of it. I find the closest jewelry shop on my phone and make my way there. Pulling into the parking lot, I decide to call Anna Mae, wanting to hear her voice.

"Hey, Royce. Is everything okay?" She answers, and everything feels right in my world again.

"Yeah, just a rough day at the store. The owner wasn't there, and I had to deal with his daughter. I'll tell you all about it tonight. How's your day going?"

"It's a bit slow. Megan says everyone has been stopping by the vet clinic to see the horse that showed up. Hank has started to allow them to peek their heads in and take a look since she's calm and healing well."

"Ahhh, tomorrow they'll all be back sharing and comparing their stories." I laugh at how predictable Rock Springs is.

"Yep, so we're enjoying a bit of downtime now."

"Okay, well, have a good day, and I have a surprise for you when you get home."

"Ahhh, I love your surprises!" Anna Mae perks right up.

"I love you, sweet girl. See you soon."

Feeling so much better, after hearing her voice, I head into the jewelry store.

"Hello, sir. How can I help you today?" A gentleman in a suit greets me.

"I'm looking for wedding rings for both my wife and me. We got married a few weeks ago spur of the moment, and I want to replace this cheap one." I say, holding up my hand.

"Okay, let's start down here. We normally carry the most common sizes in stock, but if it's not a stock size, we might have to resize one, so it could take a few days." He says.

Shoot. Ring size. I text Megan, asking her to try and get Anna Mae's ring size from her, and she texts me back that the wedding ring she's wearing is a seven. I make a mental note to ask her about my wedding day because I still don't know any of the details.

"Did you have anything in mind?" He asks once we reach the case filled with diamond rings.

"Well, she's a hairdresser and likes to wear jewelry, so I want it to stand out, but not be too big that it would be in the way with her working," I say, as I look at the rows and rows of rings.

"What about the three-piece interlocking set? She can take the big diamond band off if needed and still have both the other bands there with just as much bling." He says.

The moment I lay my eyes on the ring, it screams Anna Mae. It's small enough she can work with it on, but big enough to draw attention to any guy trying to talk to her. I can see it on her finger.

"That's the set I can see her wearing."

"Perfect, do you know her ring size?" He asks.

"Seven," I say, as I start looking over the men's wedding bands.

He disappears into the back room and comes out a moment later.

"Good news! We have it in her size." He says as he wraps it up.

"Can I see that one?" I point to a brushed metal ring for myself, as he makes his way back to me.

"Oh, you'll love this one. It's very comfortable." He says, and we chat a bit more. I do love the first ring, and they have my size.

I pay for the rings and head out to my truck. That was easier than I expected it to be, and now, she will have a real ring on her finger. One that's worthy of her.

Once I'm on my way home again, I start thinking about dinner. I know Anna Mae loves a good steak, so I plan to prepare a steak dinner. I decide to be upfront about Tara and tell Anna Mae since it's what led me to buy the rings.

As soon as I get home, I shower and change my clothes to get the last traces of Tara off me. I feel so much better. I start dinner, and I'm just finishing setting the table when I hear her car pull in.

"Hey, baby. How was your day?" I greet her at the door.

"Slow, but good. Whatever you're cooking smells amazing." She sighs.

"Steak. Come sit down. It should be almost done." I lead her to the table and then check on dinner.

As we eat, she tells me about her day and about a few of the ladies, who stopped in.

"How did it go in Dallas?" She asks.

"Well, my shelves were empty, so that was nice to see. Got the new items up, but I had to deal with the shop owner's daughter who was... a bit handsy. She tried asking me out to lunch, but I shut her down. Then I realized, we were both still wearing these cheap rings from Vegas."

Anna Mae has been quiet, but she looks down at her hand and sighs. I stand and walk to her chair and get on one knee in front of her.

"I know neither of us remembers our wedding day, but that doesn't mean you shouldn't have a proper ring," I say, pulling the wedding band set from my pocket.

I slide her ring off and look her in the eyes, as I put the new set on.

"I promise to always be here for you, take care of you, love you, and be your best friend and family for the rest of my life."

Then, I pull my ring out of my pocket and hold it out to her. Hoping she will want to do the same, and my heart swells, when she takes it from me.

She slides the ring off my hand and replaces it with the new one.

"I promise to always be here for you, to be your best friend, to laugh with you, to cry with you, and to always give you as much of me as I can." She whispers the last part, and I know what it means for her to say it.

I lean in and pull her down for a kiss. She locks her arms around my neck and deepens the kiss. Still on my knee, I slide my hands up her legs, until I get to the top of her thighs, then lift them and wrap her legs around my waist, picking her up in a quick movement that makes her giggle.

Her giggling, while she buries her head in my neck, makes my heart race. I love that sound, and I need to make her do it more often.

I sit us down on the couch, and she moves, so she's straddling me and looking into my eyes. Neither of us says a word, as she studies my face, and without warning, she grinds against my cock, which was already semi-hard, but with one shift of her hips, it's now hard as steel.

She does it again, and I close my eyes, throwing my head back. It feels so good, the sensations washing over me. When I open my eyes, her face is so close to mine, and the need to kiss her takes over. I have to kiss her now, or I feel like I might die.

I wrap my hand down around the back of her neck and pull her in. As my lips crash against hers, she starts a steady rhythm of grinding on me. She increases her thrusts, so I trail my hands down her body to her hips to slow her down just a little.

"Nice and steady, sweet girl," I mumble against her lips.

"Royce..." She gasps.

"I know, and I'll always take care of my wife. I know what you need."

I may be inexperienced, but I wanted to make sure I knew what I was doing, so I had a very uncomfortable talk with Jason about some basic bedroom techniques and demanded he use any name, but my sisters. I then did my own research online, staying as far away from porn as I could, per Jason's suggestion. I wanted to make sure I could satisfy Anna Mae, knowing that since we were married, this time would come.

I love these long, flowy skirts she wears to work. Right now, it makes it easy to run my hands up underneath and find her lace panties. Can she hear my heart pounding? This will be the first time I get to touch her like this, that I can remember anyway. Anything could have happened in Vegas on our wedding night.

I rub my thumb over the soaked panties, finding just the right spot when she gasps my name again. This time I slide her panties aside and find her clit, rubbing circles around it slowly but firmly.

Her movements become irregular, and she has a death grip on my shoulder. I know she's close, and with a little maneuvering, I'm able to continue stoking her clit and move a finger inside of her. She's so wet, and I can feel her pulsing around my finger.

I can't wait to feel that around my cock, but I will wait as long as she needs because I want that with her.

"Royce," she moans and throws her head back.

With the long, slender column of her neck on display, and her beautiful full breasts bouncing with each stroke, I'm so close to cumming I need to get her there. I pick up the pace on her clit, and it only takes a few strokes, before she clamps down on my fingers and screams my name.

Her orgasm coats my fingers, as I slowly keep thrusting them in and out of her to prolong her orgasm. I'm so concentrated on her that I'm caught off guard, when she grinds even harder down on me, causing my own climax. It's so powerful my eyes close, as I moan her name.

When I open my eyes again, she's watching me, as we both are trying to catch our breath.

"You're beautiful when you cum." She whispers.

I pull my hand from her, bringing the fingers that were just inside her to my mouth, never breaking eye contact with her, as I lick them clean.

"You taste better than anything I could have imagined. I'm addicted to you." I tell her, and the flush on her face deepens. I lean in and give her a soft kiss.

"You've had a long day. Let's get you to bed."

We may be going to separate beds tonight, but it's still the best night of my life. *That I can remember.*

Chapter 9

Anna Mae

Tonight is date night, and we are going to the concert at WJ's in town. Other than the horse that was abandoned at Mike and Lilly's, the concert is all anyone in town has been talking about. The band has been doing stops all over Texas and drummed up a big name for themselves.

I've been taking my time doing my hair and getting ready to go. I figured I'd keep it casual with boots, jeans, and a flannel shirt. I decided to style my hair and put on makeup, since it's date night, and as I'm finishing my makeup, the light catches my ring.

I've gotten so many compliments on it since Royce put it on my hand. He knew just what to say, too. The vows he made were exactly what I needed to hear. They are just what I need right now. He hasn't tried to push for more than I can give, and that alone makes me want to try harder.

I wasn't too happy to hear about that Tara girl, but he promised next time he goes up, I can go with him. He insisted on it. The fact that he told me upfront about it calms my nerves. Liam would have laughed it off, and though he was hot shit for having a girl hit on him like that.

Recently, Royce admitted to how uncomfortable she made him. He was nervous to tell me about it, because of my past, but I'm glad he did. It wasn't a big deal, but it would have hurt so much if he had tried to keep it from me.

I take a deep breath and make my way out to the living room. Royce is on his phone, probably texting Ella, I'm sure. They have been texting nonstop since she announced she's pregnant. He's always checking on her, making sure she has everything she needs, and asking about her doctor's appointments. If he's this great at being an uncle, I can only imagine him as a dad, and I've been trying not to imagine that because it makes me want things I can't have.

When I clear my throat, Royce looks up, and his eyes rake over me. They pause just a moment longer on the ring on my finger before they take in the rest of me. He loves having his ring there. At night on the couch, he will hold my hand and just rub the ring. I don't think he even realizes he's doing it.

"You look amazing, sweetheart." He says, as his eyes make a second pass, looking me over again.

He's wearing dark jeans, boots, and a light blue, button-down shirt with his cowboy hat.

"You look pretty damn good yourself, cowboy." I smile at him.

He gives me one of his half grins, and something about it is sexy as hell. He takes my hand, and we make our way to his truck. Always the perfect gentleman, Royce opens my door and helps me in, before getting in his side and heading into town.

Once at WJ's, my nerves start to hit. This is the first time we will be out in town together since we got married. Part of me is nervous, but a bigger part is excited to stake my claim tonight.

He pulls me close, wrapping his arm around my waist, as we walk to the back, where Jason is tending bar.

"Hey, I'm glad you two made it. I saved you a seat." Jason says and leads us to a small table with a reserved sign on it.

When we're seated, I lean in and ask, "What did you do to earn a reserved table? I've never seen him do that for anyone."

He shrugs, "I'm family and mentioned I was bringing you in to show you off tonight, and he wanted to help." Royce says as he picks up my hand. "Don't bother looking at the menu. Nick has a few of your favorites ready for us."

Of course, he does. I shouldn't expect anything else from a date with Royce. He knows how to make me feel cared about. For someone to put in this much effort into making me happy, is all I ever wanted. Why couldn't I find Royce first?

As we eat, we talk about our week, our childhoods, and things our siblings did. We talk about our parents and his church back in Tennessee.

Then, I notice the new guy at the bar, looking over at us. Royce follows my line of sight, and when the guy notices Royce, he nods his head and turns back around.

"Something about him gives me the creeps," I say, as a shiver runs down my spine.

Just then, Kelli walks over and sits next to him, tossing her long, blonde hair over her shoulder. They start talking and flirting.

"Rumor at the shop is they're hooking up." I nod in their direction.

"Yeah, I've been hearing that, too. I think they're perfect together, honestly."

I laugh because it's true. They seem to be a good match. Both only care about themselves and are just looking for some fun here and there.

As the band gets going and starts playing, more and more people get up and dance.

"Dance with me?" Royce asks.

"You know how to dance?" I ask.

"Not great, but good enough. Ella wanted to learn to dance, before her wedding, so we watched some videos online and practiced together." He says, as he stands up and takes my hand, leading me onto the dance floor.

He pulls me close, and we start swaying to the music. With my body so close to his, every nerve ending is on fire. He rests his head next to mine and whispers in my ear.

"I really like you pressed up against me like this." He says as he pulls me a little closer, so I can feel his hard length pressed against my belly.

"I like it, too," I whisper back.

When the song changes to a faster one, he spins me around the dance floor, making me laugh. Seeing the pure happiness on his face is worth everything. I decide right then and there to do my best to put that smile on his face every day. He looks so handsome and carefree in this moment.

We stay for the entire show and laugh, talk, and dance. We eat entirely too much food and neither of us has even a sip of alcohol, but we seem to be having more fun than anyone else there.

A few people come and congratulate us on getting married. Some want to know how it happened; others want to know if what they heard was true. I guess it's my grandma who has been spreading our Vegas wedding around town. She has also kept her distance and been pretty quiet since we all got back.

Once the band wraps up, we get ready to leave.

"I'm not sure I'm ready for the night to end," I say.

"Then I have an idea," Royce says, pulling me to his side, and we head out. Once we get home, he drives past the house to a little dirt road, along the fence line, and a few minutes later, we are in the field we had the picnic at.

He drives to the center of the field and parks the truck. He turns the radio on and opens the back, truck window, before coming around to help me out. We walk to the back of the truck, and opening the tailgate, he picks me up and sets me on it.

I fall back and dangle my feet, looking at the stars.

"It's so beautiful out here. You can't see the stars like this in Dallas. When I first moved out here, I spent the first week outside every night, looking at the stars. Not only did it make my problems feel small, it was therapeutic. Even now, on the most stressful days, I can just look up there, and it calms me." I say.

I turn my head and look over at Royce, who has laid down next to me. His eyes search my face before he leans up and kisses me. A soft, short kiss that's enough for the butterflies in my belly to flutter around.

"I love sitting on the back porch and watching the sunset and the stars come out. One of the things that sold me on the house was that back porch. Maybe tomorrow night, you'd sit out there with me?" He asks.

"I'd like that," I say, taking his hand.

When a slow song comes on the radio, Royce stands in the back of the truck and tugs me up to him. Pulling me close, we start swaying to the music, standing in the bed of his truck.

All the same feelings from earlier tonight, when he was pressed against me, come back. Feeling every move he makes, sparks shoot up and down my body. His warm breath hitting my ear sends tingles down my spine and makes my heart race, as he sings the song to me, telling me how much he loves me.

"This is the perfect ending to tonight," I tell him when the song is over. He still hasn't let me go, and I don't want him, too. As the next song starts, I rest my head on his shoulder.

He pulls me in even closer and runs his hands up my back.

"I love you just like this. Carefree, pressed against me, and happy." He says.

I know exactly what he means. It's like we were both able to let our walls down tonight and just be Royce and Anna Mae, and not the couple that got married, while drunk in Vegas, and now has to figure everything out. We got to be just us on a date the way it should have been.

The way I could have had it if I had given him a chance before Las Vegas. Something about being married gives me an extra layer of security, while at the same time scaring me.

As we wrap up the night and head back to the house, I study Royce in the moonlight. He does look so much more relaxed tonight, and even more handsome if that's possible. Every day, Royce is hot as hell with all his muscles and curly hair. But date night Royce dressed up looks like something off one of those cowboys pin up calendars.

Just as we park in front of the house, a light rain starts, and we run for the front porch, laughing the whole way. Once inside, I close the door behind us, and the second I turn to face him, he has me pressed up against the door.

His lips crash on mine, and his hands trail down my sides to my ass, pulling me up off the ground. I wrap my arms around his neck and my legs around his waist, as he pins me to the door.

His hard length grinds into me, giving me enough friction to make me gasp.

"I loved every second of you pressed against me tonight. I could tell you loved it, too. I'm not going to push you, but if at any point you want to take things further, you're always welcome in my bed. I'd be more than happy to take care of you." He nips at my ear.

Then, he sets me down, takes my hand, and walks me to my door. The entire way my body is screaming to have him pressed against me again, and for him to rush me to his bedroom and take care of me, damn the consequences. He kisses me on the cheek. "Good night, my wife." He says, before heading across the house to his room.

I walk into my room, close the door behind me, and collapse on it.

What the hell just happened?

Chapter 10

Royce

I'm sitting in the office, where I should be updating my website and posting some of my work from this week on social media, but I can't take my eyes off my wife. She's curled up in the desk chair I got her, wearing one of my sweatshirts with her dark brown hair pulled up in a messy bun, showing off her slender neck. She's watching some videos on a new coloring technique Jill wants done on her hair.

She's only in sweatpants and one of my shirts, but she looks so comfortable and relaxed. Plus, she's in one of *my* shirts, and seeing that kind of mark on her makes it impossible to take my eyes off her. She's taking notes, and I've noticed, when she's concentrating, she bites her lower lip. It's a turn on, and I've been fighting a hard-on for the last hour.

A phone rings, and I don't realize it's mine until she turns to look at me.

"It's Mike," I tell her, before answering.

"Hey, Mike," I answer.

"Hey, are you busy? We could use some help fixing up a stall for the new horse. Hank said he should be able to come home in a day or two, which is sooner than we expected."

He's talking about the horse that was dropped off at his place. It's the third horse to be found drugged but alive. Sadly, they are no closer to catching this illegal rodeo, than they were a few months ago.

"Yeah, I can be there within an hour," I tell him.

"Thanks. Miles, the state trooper, is on his way over, too. He wants to see if he can find anything tying the three horses together that they might have missed."

"Alright, see you soon." We say our goodbyes, and I turn to Anna Mae.

"I'm heading over to Mike and Lilly's. The third horse is doing better than they expected and will be home in a day or two, and they need some help fixing up the stall for it. Want to come with me?" I ask her.

I want nothing more than for her to come and spend more time with me. I love when we are in my truck together, because I get to hold her hand the whole way.

"I wish I could, but I need to finish my research here. But I'll have dinner waiting for you, when you get home." She stands up and kisses me on the cheek.

I wrap my arms around her waist, pulling her in for a real kiss on the lips. When her hands tangle in my hair, and she pulls me closer, I groan.

"Don't start something you can't finish," I tell her.

She gives me an evil smile, before sitting back down.

"Hurry up. The sooner you go, the sooner you can get home."

On the drive over to Mike and Lilly's, I can't seem to wipe the smile off my face. It was such a normal thing other married couples do, a typical conversation, but it's everything I have been waiting for with her. It's what my sisters have found, and I didn't want to admit, but I was jealous as hell. I'm extremely happy for them, but I wanted what they have so badly.

While this isn't exactly how I pictured it, I'm loving it. Coming home to her and having dinner with her, snuggling on the couch after dinner, and then enjoying coffee on the back porch in the morning. I try to soak up every minute of it.

Pulling into Mike and Lilly's, it's a flurry of activity. I head down and park by the barn and go on the hunt to see where I'm needed.

"Hey, Royce!" Lilly greets me.

"What's going on?" I ask.

"Well, Hank is here talking with Miles, and he's going over all the horses, trying to find anything linking them together. He's also reviewing the tapes and both sites here on the ranch to see if they've missed anything."

"Anything linking them?" I ask her.

"Nothing other they all had the same type of drug in them when they were found. Doesn't even look like the same scars." She shakes her head with a frown. "Sage is here helping me work with Snow and Black Diamond. Colt is helping Mike in the back stall, where you're needed."

I tip my hat to her. "On my way."

I make my way down the stalls and find the guys, where Lilly said I would.

"Hey," I say.

"Hey! Jason is coming, too. I'm hoping if we finish this stall early enough, then we might have time to get a second one completed and be ahead of the game." Mike says as they finish pulling out a rotted board.

Mike and Lilly bought this place a few months ago just before Christmas. Then, the horses started showing up, and they have been trying to do the work on the place and not upset the horses while taking in the new ones. The barn is almost done other than the stalls. They want to run a summer camp for kids here and hope to have the first round this summer.

They are now fixing up the bunkhouses that came with the property. Once completed, they'll be ready for the first batch of camp kids this summer. Their dream is to run summer camps with kids from the city. They'll teach them how to ride and take care of a horse, take them camping, and more. I guess, Mike went to a camp like it, and it made him want to be a rancher.

Ella mentioned that Sage is going to let them borrow some of their horses this summer, and by next summer, they'll be up and running. They plan to use rescue horses whenever possible.

We get to work replacing the boards that were taken down, and it's not long before Jason shows up.

"Now that we are all here, how's it going with the wife, Royce?" Mike asks.

"We're in a good place. Doing weekly dates; having a great routine. It's not quite how I imagined married life, but she's opening up slowly, so I'm willing to wait." I tell them.

"Has she told you what happened with her ex?" Jason asks.

"I know the bare bones, but we haven't talked about it. Honestly, I'm a bit scared to ask and have it set us back any." I confess.

"I only know the basics, too. She told Megan and Ella one day, and Ella shared it with me. Just enough to make me want to punch the guy's face in." Jason says.

"Amen to that. I'm not a violent person, but seeing how much he hurt her, and how much she's punishing herself for letting it happen, makes me want to punch him, too." I say, shaking my head.

We work in silence for a few minutes, before I change the subject to get my mind off Anna Mae's ex.

"So, how's Ella doing? Any morning sickness?" I ask.

A huge grin takes over Jason's face. "She's amazing. There were a few mornings where she wasn't able to eat anything, but it seems to have passed. She's been talking to Riley and Megan about their pregnancies and already planning baby names. I suggested looking at getting our own place, and she nodded. Then that night at dinner, all the girls surrounded me and said I'd take a place on the ranch or else." Jason laughs.

Ella had texted me that she doesn't want to move off the ranch, and there are plenty of cabins and old homes that would be perfect for them with a bit of work, so I knew they weren't moving.

"I'm surprised Hank is out here talking to Miles and not Hunter," I say.

Hank is Hunter's dad, and also a veterinarian, but he's now retired and only helps a few days a week in the clinic as needed. He has been working with the horses, showing up more.

"Megan had a doctor's appointment today, and she's been having some contractions, so Hunter hasn't left her side. Riley swears they're Braxton Hicks, because Megan's due date is still four weeks away." Colt says.

"Hunter's stressed. He can't do anything but support Megan. I get it. I've been thinking about it more and more." Jason says.

"Well, you know we're here for you too and not just her," I tell him, and he nods.

We move on to lighter subjects, like trying to guess what Megan is going to name her baby and also planning a guy's night the next time the girls do their girl's night.

On the drive home, all the talk of babies still lingers in my head. I'd love nothing more than to have kids with Anna Mae, but she seems to think that's out of the question. Hell, she won't even have sex with me, since our wedding night. Assuming, we even had sex on our wedding night.

She turns me on like nothing else, but I don't want to push her. I want her to know I'd wait for her as long as it takes for her to have confidence in me; to fully trust me. To me, that trust means so much more than sex or any physical part of the relationship.

There are days I wonder if she will ever trust me. Then, there are days I see her letting me in more and more. I just have to have faith in her and show how much I love her.

Pulling into the driveway, I'm firm in my belief to be patient and let her lead.

Walking into the house and smelling the delicious dinner she planned for me, I head into the kitchen and get the air knocked out of me.

The sight of Anna Mae in the kitchen no longer in the sweats she was wearing when I left the house, but in tiny cotton shorts and a tank top, reaching into the cabinet to pull down plates and cups to set the table, is a sight I will not soon forget. It'll be keeping me company tonight.

I should help her, or at the very least, let her know I'm here, but watching her stretching to reach the cups and having the bottom of her perfect ass cheek peeking out from the tiny shorts, is more than I can take. My eyes are riveted on her perfect round ass, which makes me want to reach out and grab it. When she turns around and catches me, I don't even feel sorry.

A beautiful pink stains her cheeks. "I'm sorry. I spilled something all over my clothes and changed really quick, so the food didn't burn, and then I thought I had more time to get dressed before you got home." She says as she pulls the clothes down to cover herself better.

"You're beautiful, and walking in and seeing you in this, is better than anything you can cook for me. Don't ever feel sorry for being comfortable in our home, my sweet girl. I won't ever push for more than you're ready for or willing to give, but I sure as hell like the view." I tell her, running my eyes over her again.

She gives a nervous laugh before she finishes setting the table. Over dinner, I tell her all about Miles being there and about fixing up the stable, and even about the talk of Megan and Ella's pregnancies. It feels good to share this everyday normal part of my life with her.

I meant what I said, I won't ever force her for more than she's ready to give, but I send up a silent prayer because my dick doesn't seem to have gotten the message.

Chapter 11

Anna Mae

I'm woken up by my phone ringing. I roll over and look at the clock on my nightstand. It's four a.m. Who the hell is calling me at four in the morning?

I reach for my phone, not looking at my nightstand, and I hear a few books hit the floor before I find my phone.

"Hello?" I ask

"I'm so sorry to wake you, but I'm in labor and heading to the hospital. Please, call Jill and Maggie!" Megan says.

"Shit! Okay, I'm up, and we're on our way," I say, as I sit up in bed.

"Oh, no need, too. Just make sure Jill takes care of the shop, and everyone who I promised to let know knows."

"Funny you think that waiting room isn't going to be packed? Go, we'll be there."

She huffs, and then a contraction hits, as Hunter is in the background, telling her to breathe and asking if he should pull the truck over.

"So, help me God, if you stop this truck, I will rip your balls off, so I never have to go through this again!" Megan screams at him.

"Megan, I'm hanging up to make the calls. Breathe and text me if you need anything!" I say and hang up.

I need to wake up Royce, but I've never been into his room, while he's in there, much less sleeping.

Making my way to his room, I find his door cracked open. Then saying a silent prayer that at least it's not locked, I walk quietly to his side of the bed and look at him. No shirt and his tan, muscular shoulders are on full display, and I take a moment to commit this moment to memory. Then, I steal my nerves to wake him.

"Royce," I say and place my hand on his shoulder and shake him. He starts to stir, so I do it again. "Royce."

This time he rolls to his back and his eyes open. They focus on me, and for a moment, I forget why I'm even in here. It's enough time for him to wrap his hand around my waist and flip me over him and into the bed beside him. I let out a squeal at the unexpected movement.

"What do you need, my wife?" He asks, as he buries his head in my neck and starts placing light kisses there.

"Royce." I moan, as his kisses start trailing down to my chest. It all feels so good I can't remember why I'm in here, and what I needed from him. I wrap my arms around his neck and hold him close, as he kisses back up the other side of my neck.

"Yes, baby?" He asks in his husky voice.

Baby.

Then, it all comes back to me.

"Royce, Megan," I say, still not able to pull away from his kisses.

When he stops, he looks into my eyes.

"What?" He asks.

"Megan called. She's in labor. She wanted us to call Maggie, and we should get going to the hospital." I tell him.

He groans and rolls off me. I have to say, I agree with his small protest. I'm already missing the loss of his body heat.

"Go get ready, sweet girl. I'll call Maggie and meet you at the truck."

Deciding to be brave and open up a little bit, I roll towards him, and before I can second guess myself, I kiss him. Without missing a beat, his hands are in my hair, as he takes control of the kiss.

I don't realize I've climbed and straddled him, until his hands are on my waist, stopping me from grinding against him.

"Baby, I want you, don't get me wrong." He says as he thrusts his hips up, and I can feel how hard he is against me. "But we have to get going."

I sigh and sit up, giving him one more roll of my hips, causing us both to moan, before I climb off him and the bed.

"Evil girl." He says with a smile on his face, as I leave the room.

As I'm changing, I call Jill.

"Someone better be dead." She answers, her voice full of sleep.

"Megan's in labor," I say.

"Anna Mae?" She asks.

"Yeah, Megan just called."

"Shit, she's early," Jill says, her voice a little clearer now.

"Yeah, she's thirty-six weeks and a few days."

"Okay, well, I'll open the shop. I'm assuming you're going to the hospital?" She asks.

I head out to Royce's truck now that I'm dressed.

"Yeah, Ella will be, too."

"So, it's just me."

"And you know no one will care when you have all the news of what's going on right from Ella and me."

"I know, the tips are going to be amazing today." I can hear the smile in her voice. "You send pictures as soon as you can, and I'll split tips with you. The ladies will go crazy to get the first photos."

"If Megan says I can, you have a deal. We're leaving now for the hospital, and I'll let you when I know something."

We hang up, as I'm climbing into Royce's truck that he has warmed up already.

"That was Jill. She's opening on her own today," I tell him.

"Maggie and Nick are on their way, too." He tells me. The moment he puts the truck in gear, his hand goes to mine and holds it the whole way there.

"You seem tense." He says about halfway to the hospital.

"Megan's early by almost a month," I say. That seems to be all I have to say, because he squeezes my hand, and we go back to listening to the radio.

When we walk in, he leads me to the family waiting room. He was here recently when Riley had baby Lilly. When we get there, the family takes up over half the waiting room. Megan's parents, Hunter's parents, and Royce's parents are there. So are Riley and Blaze with baby Lilly, Sage and Colt, Jason and Ella, Mac and Sarah, Lilly and Mike, and Maggie and Nick.

Before we even get to sit down, a nurse comes in, and when she sees all of us, she stops in her tracks.

"Are all of you family of Megan and Hunter?" She asks in shock.

"Yes." We all say at the same time.

The nurse smiles and shakes her head.

"Well, she's asking for her mom and Hunter's mom."

The moms follow the nurse back, promising updates as they have it.

"Did we miss anything?" Royce asks as we sit down, and he pulls me up to his side.

"Not really. She was admitted and is having the baby. The doctor said they gave her a boost of something for the baby's lungs, but she's so close to thirty-seven weeks, which they consider full term that there's no point in stopping it now, especially since she's measuring a little big," Megan's dad, Tim, says.

Not twenty minutes later, everyone's phone goes off with a text from Megan's Mom.

Helen: She's already six cm. Baby is coming fast!

"So, are we taking guesses on the name?" Riley asks.

Though Riley, Megan, and Hunter know what the baby's name is, they haven't shared it with anyone.

Everyone gives their guesses, and the room is pretty much split, and no one agrees. They all start talking about the time when it was Riley giving birth just a few short months ago.

An hour after her last text, Helen texts again.

Helen: She's getting ready to push!

"Wow, she wasn't kidding about the baby coming fast," Riley says.

The next hour is a blur, as Megan's baby girl makes her way into the world. Her name is Willow, and she's a healthy seven pounds. The name has a special meaning to them, but they haven't said what. Each couple goes back one by one to see Megan and Hunter and meet the new baby girl.

It's finally our turn, as we follow Megan's mom back to the room. For just giving birth, Megan looks amazing. She's glowing and all smiles.

"You look amazing, Megan," I say and watch, as Royce takes baby Willow from Hunter.

I can't take my eyes off him. He knows exactly how to hold the baby and is lightly bouncing her and talking to her like she knows exactly what he's saying. The smile on his face is so large that for a moment I wish that it was our baby in his hands. That I could give a baby to him, because he's going to make a great father, and I don't want to take the opportunity from him.

"So, tell me the story behind her name." I turn to Megan, as I try to clear those thoughts from my head.

"When I graduated with my business degree, Hunter took me on a vacation right before I took over the shop. We went to Sedona, Arizona, and the cabin he rented was called The Willow Canopy. It's where we started the romantic part of our relationship, and we had many firsts in that cabin." Megan says, her cheeks turning pink.

"Before I forget, Jill wants a photo to share with all the ladies at the shop," I tell her.

"I knew she would, so I sent her one a little bit ago." Megan smiles.

"Here, sweetheart, take a turn with the baby." Royce hands me Willow, and it's hard not to get lost in her sweet face. Her perfect little hand reaches out and grabs hold of my finger, as she snuggles into me.

My heart clenches, as I look up at Royce, and I can't quite read the look on his face. I want this, not just the family and extended family we are here with today, but a family of our own.

I have to get out of the hospital, so I turn and paste on a smile for Megan and Hunter.

"She's absolutely beautiful," I tell them, as I hand her back to him. "We should get going. I want to go in and help Jill. Once word gets out you had the baby, the shop will be packed."

"Oh, yes, it will. Feel free to share photos and the name. It's not like it will stay a secret for long." Megan laughs.

Royce takes my hand, as we head out to the car. He talks about how cute Willow is, and how sweet it was for them to name her after a place that holds such a special meaning.

I don't say a word on the way home, as I'm lost in thought. Is there a way to make what we have work and maybe have a family? What if things don't work out? What about the kids then? I don't want my kids growing up like that. But am I willing to give up the chance at having kids all together?

The thought of Royce and I not making it and splitting up hurts, as much as the thought of never having any kids. I'm a mess. How he puts up with me I will never know.

I don't even realize the entire drive has passed, until he parks in the driveway. He helps me out of the truck, and once inside, he pulls me over to the couch and onto his lap.

"Are you okay? You didn't say a word on the way home. I don't think you even heard anything I said." He asks me, his voice soft.

Since I know the key to any good relationship is communication, I know I have to talk to him.

"I'm sorry," I start.

"You don't need to apologize. Please, talk to me and let me help you with whatever is bothering you." He says as he rubs my back.

I sigh, "You're going to make a great father."

He gives me one of his half grins that make my heart skip a beat.

"I just feel like I'm holding you back from that, and I don't see kids in my future anymore." I tell him honestly.

"Your vision of the future is constantly changing. A few months ago, did you see yourself married to me?" He asks.

"Well, no," I say.

"Now look into your future. Do you see yourself *not* married to me?" He asks a bit of uncertainty in his voice.

"No, I don't want to picture my future different than it is right now."

"See, you're healing, and that takes time. Trust takes time."

"What if I wanted to change up our relationship a little bit?" I ask.

Pictures of this morning, flash into my mind, and that alone is enough to turn me on. I want to take it further. *I want him.*

"What do you mean?" He asks.

"Well, what if I wanted to add sex to it?" I ask bluntly. Rip off the Band-Aid and get it out there.

"I don't remember our first time." He says a bit hesitantly.

"Me either. If anything even happened, anyway." I say.

"We are married." He says.

"But not in the way you want that would make you go along with this." I finish his thought for him.

He gives me another one of those sexy half grins, and I can't take it. I lean in and kiss him, just a soft, chaste touch, before pulling away.

He looks torn, and I send up a silent prayer he agrees, because that smile alone is going to make my ovaries explode.

Chapter 12

Just this conversation alone has me rock hard. There's one thing I want almost as much as I want sex with my wife, and that's my wife in our bed every night.

"Under one condition," I say, my voice huskier than I intended.

"What?" She whispers.

I stand up and carry her to our room, placing her in the middle of the bed.

"You move in here with me. Move into our room, and spend every night in our bed." I say.

"Royce..." She breathes, but I go for broke.

"Move in here, so I can love you, as my wife. Make sure you go to bed satisfied every night and wake you with an orgasm every morning."

She groans, and I see the tight peaks of her nipples, brushing against her thin shirt. She wants to agree, but she's holding herself back.

So, I lean down and kiss each nipple over her shirt.

"Say yes, sweet girl," I say, trailing kisses down her stomach.

"Royce..." She groans again.

I get to the top of her pants and pull away, making her whimper.

"Say yes, and I'll give you the relief you need. Now and always." I let my eyes plead with her.

"Yes." She says.

"Yes, what?" I ask, needing to be sure.

"Yes, I'll move in here with you."

"If you need to call Jill, now's your chance, because we aren't leaving this room today," I tell her.

No way I can let her go to work now. No chance to change her mind and no way will once be enough.

When she sits up and pulls me to her, I let her lead for just a bit. She pulls my shirt off, and then brings her mouth to mine, as she starts kissing me. Fair is fair, so I pull her shirt off and continue kissing her.

Being skin to skin with her is an experience I want to have every day. I run my hands up and down her soft skin, as I kiss her and soak it all in. I unhook her bra, and then stand up, unbuttoning my pants.

The zing of the zipper fills the air before my pants fall to the ground. Standing in just my boxer briefs, I take in the sight of my wife on our bed; her sex glistening in need of me. I make quick work of removing her pants and underwear.

Letting my gaze continue to roam over her, she's the most beautiful thing I've ever seen. When she tries to close her legs and cover herself, I stop her.

"You're perfect, don't hide from me," I whisper, and it stops her in her tracks. I remove my boxer briefs and kneel down in front of the bed, pulling her ass to the edge.

I run my finger through her soaking wet folds. This isn't the first time my hand has been here, but it's the first time I get to see her up close, and my God, she's perfect.

For the first time, I run my tongue down her folds, and her hips try to buck off the bed. Her hands tangle in my hair, pulling me closer, and I love it, as I double my efforts.

I insert a finger into her and feeling how warm and wet she is, I try not to think about it wrapped around my cock, or I'm going to cum before I even get into her.

She starts grinding on my face, as I insert a second finger. I latch on to her clit and give it a firm suck, and she clenches down on my finger, screaming my name. I continue to, as her orgasm pulses around me.

I'm so on edge, and I don't know how I held on this long. I reach into the nightstand for a condom, when she grabs my hand.

"I'm on the pill and was checked after... everything, and I haven't been with anyone since." She says to me.

I have trouble swallowing.

"What are you saying, sweet girl? I need your words." I choke out.

"We don't have to use condoms, if you don't want, too. You should get the full experience your first time." She whispers the last part.

I nod and climb on the bed between her thighs, never breaking eye contact with her.

"You sure about this?" I whisper. "There's no going back. You'll be mine in every way."

"I've never been more sure of anything in my life."

That's all I need to hear, as I line my cock up with her entrance and pause, as I feel her slick entrance kiss the tip of my cock. A full body shudder goes through me before I slide into her.

I'm not even all the way in and have to stop and catch my breath. There are no words to describe the first time sliding into my wife. She's warmer, wetter, and tighter than anything I could have imagined.

She rocks her hips, signaling me to move, so I start with slow quick thrusts, until she's taking all of me, and I'm already ready to come, but I refuse to go over unless she goes with me.

"I need you to cum, sweet girl. You feel too good, and I'm not going to last," I mumble against her neck, reaching my hand between us and start rubbing her clit.

Her hips buck, as she meets me thrust for thrust. I lean down and suck one of her nipples into my mouth, and thankfully, it's enough to make her climax, screaming my name. Two more short thrusts and I'm following her over the edge.

I cum so hard and so violently that all my muscles lock up, and I swear for a moment I can't even breathe. As I come down from the high, I collapse on top of her. I couldn't stop myself if I tried.

As soon as I gain control of my muscles again, I move us to our sides, though not pulling out of her. I run my hand through her hair, as we hold each other close.

I know for her this is just sex. Just friends with benefits, but I can't lie. For me, this is so much more.

As we lay connected, there's a new bond that we did not have before, and I know she feels it, too.

Not to mention, it was mind-blowing. But holding her in my arms now, as we cuddle in bed afterward, is a very close second. Completely skin to skin all her walls down, the outside world can't touch us here.

"I didn't know sex could be like that." She says.

"Like what?" I ask as I run my hand up and down her silky, smooth arm.

"So... intimate. I know I was the one who said friends with benefits, and I hope this doesn't scare you off, but I don't think I've ever connected with someone like that." She says while running her hands over my chest.

"You can't scare me off. If anything, it will be me scaring you off. And your ex sounds like an idiot," I say.

I feel her smile, as she turns her head to kiss my chest. She shifts a bit, and I slip out of her, as she turns and rests her head on my shoulder.

"We met in college, and I didn't know any better. He graduated two years before me, and by the time I graduated, he had a life started for us, as he would say, and I was blinded by what could be."

I've been asking her to open up about her ex for a while now, so I'm scared to even breathe in case it makes her change her mind.

"He proposed at my graduation, and we were married six weeks later. From the moment we got back from the honeymoon, and I moved in, it was all work. I knew he was making a name for himself and had just gotten a promotion a few months before, so I made excuses."

She pauses, and I pull her close to me, not that there was any extra space between us to begin with.

"He would get up and have breakfast with me, but he wasn't with me. He would have already read the paper and didn't like me talking. Then, he'd rush off to work. Most nights he'd be home just in time for dinner, lock himself in his office all night, and then come to bed for sex. Both of us would pass out, or he would go back to work. He was so excited when I said I wanted to go to cosmetology school. I had a business degree though, and I could help manage a salon or spa. Now, I guess he was excited because it would keep me busy and distracted."

I kiss the top of her head. Just something to let her know I'm here, and I'm listening.

"It worked for a bit, and I was happy in school. Made some new friends and got a job at a nice salon. On weekends, I was his arm candy to show off at work events and played the part of his wife well. The less time we spent together, the happier I got. By the time I got my cosmetology license, sex was almost nonexistent, and we had barely been married a year. Our dating anniversary came up, and I thought this was a good time to get the spark back. It worked for a bit, and he spent a little more time at home, but things went back to the old way fast."

She pauses, lost in thought, as I run my hand up and down her back, trying to offer her comfort.

"I guess, I knew in the back of my mind he was cheating on me, but I was so happy in my life, minus him, that I didn't care. I didn't think about it. Then one day, he took my car to work, so I could use his SUV to move boxes to our storage unit on my day off. I got done early and thought I'd go in for a half-day at work. I needed my car because it had my parking pass for the lot, so I went to switch it out, didn't call or anything, and walked in on him fucking his secretary over his desk from behind. The worst part? When he saw it was me, he didn't even stop."

"What an asshole," I say, unable to stay silent anymore.

"Funny, those are the exact words that crossed my mind. I saw my keys on the coffee table in his office, and I switched them out. Told him I'd be gone, before he got home. I called my grandma on the way and asked if I could store some stuff at her place until I figured out what to do. She said I could come live with her, and she told me about Megan having an open spot in the salon, so I took the chance. I packed everything into my car, and it fit thankfully, and I left my house key and my rings on the kitchen counter and left. I called Megan the next day and got the job."

She gives an almost sarcastic chuckle. "Then I filed for divorce. He was willing to sign the papers pretty fast and took pleasure in rubbing it in my face that his secretary was pregnant. I wasn't surprised, honestly. What better way to keep a married man than to get knocked up? Anyway, the day I got my final divorce papers, and the money for the divorce showed up in my account, my grandma and I got drunk. Like worse than I was in Vegas drunk, and I don't remember the whole weekend, but her friends come over and told me stories. Apparently, I described in detail what they were doing on his desk. I also laid out in detail how horrible he was in the bedroom, and they loved every minute. The next week I met you, so you can understand why dating was the last thing on my mind."

"Have you talked to him since?"

"Nope, don't know about the baby or anything. I did report him to his boss, and I know he got in trouble for that right before the divorce was final, but I cut off contact with everyone I knew there because they all know him. Even the girls at the salon and their husbands became friends with him, so I cut them all out, too. Megan took me under her wing, and she's now one of my closest friends."

"What did your family do, when all this happened?"

"Mom and Dad were on my side, but they made it very clear I needed to handle it on my own, as they are too busy working. Grandma was my biggest cheerleader. She still won't say his name, but she calls him the cheating bastard. My brother's wife had just had a miscarriage when all this went down. He wanted me to move in with them and help me get back on my feet, but they live in New Jersey and work in the city. I'm not a city girl, and I didn't want to be in the way."

"I hope you know you have me and my whole family, and by extension, Megan's family, since she's Ella's sister-in-law. You aren't alone, and I promise you won't be again."

"I know, but it's just hard to believe it most days." She says.

Desperate to cheer her up, I tell her, "I'm going to feed you. Why don't you take a bath and relax, while I cook?" I say as I pull on my pants, and she watches every move I make.

I take my time cooking, letting her relax in the bath, and soaking in everything she told me. She opened up to me, so I figure it's time I opened up to her as well.

After we eat, I bring her into the living room and sit down on the couch, pulling her into my lap. This is my favorite way to sit on the couch.

"My turn to share," I say.

She looks at me with curious eyes but nods her head.

"You know my family moved here from Mountain Gap, Tennessee. My parents were really big with the church there. Ella's courtship with Jason was a lot different than how Maggie and Nick were dating." I start.

"I remember Megan telling me a bit about it."

"Well, we grew up in the church, and it was very strict. The girls only wore dresses and skirts, no pants. It was very modest, but my parents weren't like the others in the church. They're sweet and soft-spoken. They didn't just tell us to do something, because they said so, they'd explain why they asked it of us. Even at an early age, we didn't date, and the church pushed courtship. Chaperoned dates with very little touching. Your first kiss is on your wedding day, and of course, no sex."

She wraps her arm around my neck and snuggles into me.

"I never thought anything of it. I didn't think it was how I wanted to raise my kids. I wasn't a huge fan of the church, but it was important to my parents, so I went every week and to any event, they asked me, too. Ella started courting Jason, and it opened up a lot of talk in our house. He wasn't someone the church would approve of. He was a bar owner, cowboy, and quite a bit older than her. My parents made it clear they wanted us to be happy and for us not to rush into a relationship, but they wouldn't rule out someone just because the church didn't agree with them. I didn't know at that time my parents were having issues with the church."

My hand moves to her cheek, as she says, "I remember the issues with Seth on Ella and Jason's wedding day. I was there helping decorate."

I nod, "Seth was the straw that broke the camel's back. The church loved him and wanted Ella to marry him, and they condemned Jason, even though he was willing to follow the courtship rules. Jason hired a private investigator to look into Seth and found out Seth wasn't his real name, and that he was wanted on many rapes and a few murder charges. My parents pretty much walked away then. Jason and Ella got married, and we all tried to make it work back home, but our whole life there was mixed with the church."

She rests her head on my shoulder, and I pull her close.

"So, one day, Mom and Dad sat Maggie and me down and asked what we thought of moving here to be near Ella. Of course, Maggie had her eye on Nick, but none of us knew that. Everyone knew I had my sights set on you, so there was no hesitation on either of our ends. When Sage offered my parents the house on the ranch, everything lined up. A week later we found someone to rent our house, and we moved."

"Just in time for Thanksgiving." She says as I smile at that memory. "Our first of many holidays together," I agree, squeezing her hip.

"Is all that why you don't go to church now? I noticed you haven't gone, since we've been back from Las Vegas."

She's right. We've been home a month, and I haven't gone once. I haven't missed it too much, even though the church here, is night and day difference, then the church back in Tennessee.

"Partly. Before we got married, I went once or twice a month. Pastor Greg is amazing, and I love the town, but now, it's more so that I don't want to give up time with you. When you're at work, I pull up some church services from the past week online, since many churches stream them live now."

"I don't want to be the reason you don't go." She says.

"I'm the reason I don't go. I want to be here with you, even if it's just us sitting in the office working together. I'm not passing up time with you. Now, if I could convince you to go with me, that would be another story." I try to joke.

"I haven't been to church, since I would visit my grandma in the summers. She never forced me after the divorce, though she did ask me every week to go with her. Maybe soon. I think I need to be in the right headspace first." She says.

"I won't ever push you, but I'm happy to take you anytime you want, just ask."

We are both quiet together, snuggled up, and my mind starts thinking about the house. She hasn't touched it or anyplace in the house. The only sign she's here are the clothes in her closet, the photos I placed out here in the living room, and her stuff in my bathroom.

"You really should start decorating this place and put your touch on it. Maybe, look into the type of kitchen you want. That's the next remodel I'd like to tackle. The kitchen isn't old, but it needs updating."

"Yeah, maybe." She brushes off the suggestion again, and I don't push.

Chapter 13

We are on our way to Dallas for our weekly date, but also to drop stuff off for consignment. Royce's stuff sold out again, and today, he's going to negotiate another shelf for his stuff.

"I'm thinking with summer coming up, maybe doing some red, white, and blue American décor, and some with the Texas flag and star. Don, the store owner, says that stuff did well last summer." Royce says.

He's holding my hand, like he does every time we get in the truck together, as he goes over his ideas for the next batch of stuff to take to the store. I think he's trying to take my mind off it because I'm a bit tense about running into this Tara girl.

The last week in his bed has been perfect. Maybe, mind-blowing is a better word. True to his word, he makes love to me every night and wakes me up every morning with an orgasm. It's a routine I'm addicted to for sure.

After I spent the first night in his bed, the next day he moved all my clothes into the second closet in his room. By that night, he had my room cleaned out and turned back into a guest room with all my stuff in our room, as he calls it.

This is how I always pictured being married. Almost every night, he stops work, when I get home and spends the evening with me. The few times he's worked late to finish an order on time, he's had me out there with him. I love those nights where he sits me on his workbench, while he's painting and working on little details.

We decide to have lunch first and make the consignment store our last stop, before heading home. There's a burger place not too far from the shop that we have both been wanting to try, since we saw it featured on the Food Network show one night.

This place is pretty busy for lunch mid-week. I guess it has to do with being on the show. They do well to highlight it on their website, and even once you get inside.

"Hey, tell me what you want, and I'll wait in line, so you can go grab us a table, yeah?" He asks.

I agree and glance at the menu, deciding to go with the Texas burger featured on the show. Picking a table off in the corner just big enough for two, I wait for him. I get lost in my thoughts, thinking of the last time I was in this area of town.

It was with the girls from the salon. We had drinks at a bar down the road to celebrate one of the girls getting engaged.

That night Liam seemed so happy I was going out, and when I got home at almost one a.m., he still wasn't home. He said he fell asleep at his desk. I didn't press, but I know now he was with his secretary, and I have a pretty good idea of what they were doing.

I'm so lost in thought that I don't realize Royce is at the table until he places his hand on my shoulder.

"Hey, you okay?" He asks.

"Sorry, just hit with a memory of the last time I was in this part of town," I say honestly.

He doesn't say anything, but I see the question in his eyes.

"We went to a bar down the street, celebrating an engagement of one of the girls at the salon, but he was out late that night, too," I admit.

"All the more reason to make some new memories. Better ones, actually. Now, look at this food. It smells amazing, so let's see if it lives up to its hype."

The food definitely lives up to its hype. Royce got a different burger, and we share bites and talk about the food, which somehow leads to stories of food Nick has made him and his family to try out for the restaurant. We both agree to go and support Nick when he's back here in Dallas to defend his championship title at the BBQ championship later this summer.

We finish our food and just stay there talking, laughing, and having a good time until a group of women walk in the door laughing.

I look up and panic, and Royce picks up on it almost immediately, as he turns to look.

"What wrong?" He asks.

"The lady in the purple dress there. That's Liam's boss's wife," I whisper.

"Okay, let's go. There's a side door behind you. Don't look back," he says, as we stand, and he wraps his arms around my waist, leading me to the door.

In the car, he starts talking about how the horses at Mike and Lilly's are doing. He doesn't harp on what just happened and isn't forcing me to talk about it, which means so much to me.

I don't stop and think. As soon as Royce stops at a traffic light, I lean over and kiss him, while he is in mid-sentence. I catch him off guard for just a minute before he kisses me back. He pulls back just as the light turns green. A few minutes later, we pull into the shop parking lot. No sooner does he put the truck in park, he's leaning over and pulling me in for another kiss.

"Let's get this over with, so we can head home. If you keep kissing me like that, we're going to grab a hotel room, because we won't make it." He says, his voice gruff, as we both catch our breath.

We each grab a box to carry inside, and he makes sure I get the smallest and lightest one. As we walk in, I look around the store. It's a cute place, selling all unique stuff right in the heart of the shopping district. At the counter, is an older gentleman with a girl, who looks to be my age.

Her appearance is out of place here in Texas, and it's more like she should be on one of those housewives shows in California on some rich guy's arm, as a trophy wife. You know fake blonde hair, fake tits, and her make up contoured so heavily that you know you wouldn't recognize her without it.

"Hey, guys. This is my wife, Anna Mae. Baby, this is Don, who owns the shop, and his daughter, Tara." His voice goes flat at the last part, and Tara picks up on it, shooting me a hard glare.

"So, this is the *wife*," Tara says, and somehow makes the word wife, sound like an insult.

Ignoring his daughter, Don perks right up. "Oh, it's nice to meet you, Anna Mae! Now Royce, what do you have for us this time?"

"More of the same and some new stuff. I have another box in the car. Be right back," he says.

Wanting some space from Tara, I smile at Don and then head off to walk up and down the aisles, seeing what else is for sale here.

I get to the end of one of the aisles, and Tara is right there glaring at me.

"I don't know what he sees in you." She eyes me up and down, and her stare makes me feel like I need a shower.

I start to get flashbacks to Liam's secretary. She never spoke to me like this, but she did look at me the same way. It's a look of disgust and a challenge rolled into one.

"It's okay. A ring doesn't scare me off. I know I can win him over. I was well on my way to doing so when you showed up."

Feeling cattiness, I've never felt before rearing up, I just laugh. "Funny, because the whole reason he moved to Texas was to be with me." I turn and head for the door.

Royce is walking in, as I reach him, and he's able to read my face. When he looks over my shoulder to Tara, I know he's putting the pieces together.

"I'm going to wait outside. I could use the fresh air." I say, walking past him. I window shop a few of the shops along the sidewalk, trying to remind myself Royce is different than Liam, and that he wouldn't cheat on me, right? Why put in all the work this last year to win me over just to cheat on me?

About twenty minutes later, Royce walks out and looks for me, worry all over his face. When he sees me, relief fills his features, and I know I need to talk to him about this.

"Ready to go?" He asks.

I nod my head and get in the truck. He tries to talk to me on the way home, but I just stare out of the window. Tara's words are playing over and over again in my head, along with the interactions I had with Liam's secretary.

It's all so similar that I start to doubt everything. The second we pull into the driveway, I'm out of the truck.

"I'm going to go for a walk," I don't even give him time to respond, as I head out to the barn.

The biggest problem is what I feel for Royce is so much stronger and more intense than anything I ever felt for Liam. Liam was safe and strong, and marrying him was the next step in our relationship. It hurt like hell when the marriage ended, but if the same thing happened with Royce? It would break me in a way I don't think I could come back from.

I walk into the barn and right to Caramel's stall. Like she knows I need the comfort, she sticks her head out, letting me hug her. Her chin rubs along my back, making me smile just a bit.

But Royce is nothing like Liam, is he?

The voice is so clear, even though, I know it was in my head, I still look around the barn to make sure I'm alone.

Royce isn't like Liam. Royce owned up to Tara flirting with him last time he was there. If he wanted to cheat on me, he sure as hell wouldn't have told me and drawn suspicion to them. He wouldn't have brought me with him if he wanted to have something going on with her.

Then, there's the time here at home. There's a night and day difference between Royce and Liam. Royce cooks for me spends the morning with me before work, and all evening with me after work. He doesn't mind cooking or cleaning, and in fact, he's done most of that, since we've been married. On my days off, he always has something planned for us.

The weekly dates alone are a nice change because Liam and I mostly stopped doing dates long before we were married, and it stopped completely once we were married.

I'm petting Caramel, trying to talk myself down, when a throat clears behind me. I look over my shoulder and see Royce.

"I know something happened with Tara, and I'm sorry I shouldn't have left you alone in the store. I didn't think she'd do anything with her dad there. She asked me if I really moved to Texas for you, and I said damn right I did, and if you left me, I'd follow wherever you go."

He takes a few steps closer but doesn't reach for me.

"It hit me on the way home how you might be comparing her to your ex's secretary, and now, you're putting walls back up, and I hate it." He takes a step closer.

"So, I called the shop and talked to Don and explained what happened last time I was there, and what I suspected happened this time based on how you were acting. I said I'd tell him when I plan to drop things off at the shop, and I don't want her there. If she is, I'll end my agreement and go elsewhere. I love Don, but I've had other shops ask to sell my stuff. Turned them down out of respect for Don, but I respect you more and will do it in a heartbeat. I also won't be going up there again without you, and next time, I won't be leaving your side."

He takes another step towards me and reaches out to take my hand.

"I thought I shut it down last time I was there, and it would be the end of it. Tell me what she said please." His eyes beg me, along with his words.

"She said a ring wouldn't stop her, and that she'd win you over. Her exact words and she made some comment about me being your wife that just made me feel dirty." I whisper it all, scared to say it and give the words life again.

"Oh, sweet girl. No." He wraps his arms around me, pulling me into him. His scent of wood and pine washes over me, as I rest my head on his chest.

"I know it's just words, and I plan to show you I mean what I say. I love *you*. I want this marriage more than I want my next breath. I love you with everything I am. Marriage is sacred to me, and I will never break my vows. That's not who I am. Everything she is, I never wanted, even before I found you. Even if there was no you, there certainly would be no her."

His words soothe me in a way I never expected. When will my insecurities stop trying to overtake me, and stop trying to ruin what Royce and I have?

Almost like he can hear my mind racing, he pulls back enough to tip my head up and locks eyes with me for just a moment, before he leans down and captures my lips with his. It works. The only thing I can think about is Royce, my sexy as sin husband.

I don't realize he's backing me up until my back hits the stall wall, and without skipping a beat, he reaches down and grabs my ass, lifting me up. I wrap my legs around his waist and my arms around his neck, as we make out like teenagers.

His lips trail down my neck to my collar bone, where he lightly nips it, before kissing back up the other side.

"Let's go inside, so I can feed you. I put one of Nick's meat loafs in before I came out here. Then, I'll spend the rest of the night proving how only your body can turn me on like this." He says as he grinds his hips into me, and his hard cock hits just the right spot, making me gasp.

After an amazing dinner, he proves over and over all night how much he loves me.

Chapter 14

Royce

It's been a few days, since our trip to Dallas, and while things are back to normal, I still feel like her walls are partially up. I'm trying to break them down, but I honestly think it's just going to take time.

I wander into the kitchen for the fourth time in the last hour and stare out the window at my wife. She's working in the garden. I'm not sure what she's doing, but Ella's been giving her a lot of pointers, and the plants that they have grown are looking good.

She's been out there several times this week, saying it's therapeutic. She won't tell me what she's working through, while out there, but my guess is that it has to do with the Dallas trip. Either Tara setting off her insecurities, or her ex's boss's wife showing up at the burger place.

A knock on the door pulls me from my thoughts. We aren't expecting anyone today, but my family never calls, when they come over. I open the door expecting Maggie, or maybe Ella, but I find Anna Mae's grandma.

"Mrs. Willow, come on in. I didn't know you were coming over," I say, as I hug her.

"Well, you'd have to be physic, because I didn't either until I was out and realized I was only a few minutes away and haven't seen either of you, since Las Vegas. The honeymoon is over, so it's time to stop ignoring family." She swats at me and sits down in the recliner.

I chuckle, "Honeymoon was over a while ago." I shake my head.

Mrs. Willow narrows her eyes at me, "You better start talking, boy."

What do I have to lose? Maybe, having Mrs. Willow on my side can help. I don't see how it can hurt right now.

I sigh, "We were making progress, and I think she's opening up, and then a wall goes right back up. She finally talked about Liam and told me what happened, even how they met. Then, we go to Dallas to drop my stuff off, and the shop owner's daughter gets into her face, trying to stake her claim or some shit, and the wall is back. I can't seem to break it down this time, no matter what I say or do."

"It hits too close to home. That girl isn't your secretary, but she's part of your work in Dallas. Anna Mae hates going to Dallas. There are too many memories there."

"Yeah, we stopped for lunch, and Liam's boss's wife walked in, so we left in a hurry. But I don't want to go to Dallas without her either. I don't want any questions in her mind. I even called the shop owner and explained what happened with his daughter. I told him it wasn't okay, and then said if I have to see her again, I'll pull my stuff and go elsewhere." I explain.

"I don't think that will help. In her mind, it's still easy to stop somewhere for a quickie, while in town. Liam did that stuff all the time. Show up late, leave places early, and had a bunch of time unaccounted for. You may work at home, but that leaves large chunks of time for you to do as you please in her eyes."

I nod and think it over. I watch Mrs. Willow look around the room. She notices a few of Anna Mae's photos, but she doesn't say anything.

"I've been asking her since we got home from Las Vegas to decorate the house; put her stamp on it, but she hasn't."

"Decorating a house and making it a home means you are putting down roots. You don't do that unless you trust you'll be there a while." Mrs. Willow says softly, and it's easy to read between the lines. Anna Mae doesn't think this is permanent.

Dallas flashes into my mind. She's still prepared for me to mess up, and for all this to just vanish. She still doesn't feel at home or feel safe with me.

"I can't win, can I?" I ask, defeated.

"I'll tell you the same thing I've been telling her. Actions speak louder than words. Just keep showing her. It will take some time, but one day, it will click for both of you. You'll see. Now, where is this granddaughter of mine? It's time I talk some sense into her."

"Good luck. She's working in the garden. Go out the back door, and you'll see her." I point towards the kitchen.

As she heads out, I wander back into the kitchen again and look out of the window. Anna Mae stands up and greets her grandma, all smiles. Smiles I haven't seen on her face in close to a week now.

I had put a bench beside the garden a few days ago, so I could sit out there with her, while she worked, even if we didn't talk. I wanted her to know I was there and not going anywhere.

Her grandma sits on the bench, and while I can't hear what they are talking about, I have an idea of how the conversation will go. Sighing, I pull myself away from the window.

I should go to my workshop and get some projects finished, but I just can't seem to get my head on right today. I decide I'm going to go at least sit at my workbench. Maybe, it will get me in the mood to work.

Before I make it to the garage door, there's another knock on the door. I don't even try to guess who it might be this time, but on the other side is Jason.

"Hey, man. Come in. Anna Mae and her grandma are in the garden out back." I let him know.

He nods and sits down.

"So, another horse showed up at the church. Pastor Greg was doing some outside work, went to the house at the back of the property for lunch, and the horse was tied to a tree in his backyard. With how wooded it is, no one saw anything, and the tracks lead out to a dirt road a mile behind the church." He says.

"I didn't even know about that road, so whoever is doing it knows the area or has canvased and gotten to know the area," I say.

"I agree, and so does Miles. They said they're bringing in more people because in addition to the horse, there were two more stolen in the area last night." Jason says.

"From anyone we know?"

"No, some small ranch closer to the highway. Miles thinks they dropped this horse and just took advantage of the opportunity on the way out of town."

"How's the horse now?" I ask.

"Same as the others. Drugged, starved, and beaten. He's in much worse shape than the other three that have shown up. They're trying to get him to the clinic, but he's having trouble standing, according to Sage."

"Damn," I say, shaking my head.

"Yeah, she doesn't think this one will make it. If they can't get him to the clinic, they can't get the tests done to find out how bad it is, or if there are any broken bones, and anything like that."

His phone goes off, and his brow furrows, as he looks at it.

"Shit. Mike wants me to come to the clinic. They got the horse there, but it isn't good. He says Lilly's a mess, and even Sage isn't keeping it together. She never gets this torn up. At least, not in front of anyone." He stands and heads towards the door.

"Want me to come with you?" I ask.

"No, fewer people there, the better. I'll call you later tonight and update you." He says, going out to his truck.

I once again make my way to the kitchen window. Anna Mae and her grandma are laughing and smiling. I know she will want to know about the horse and what Jason said, but I don't want to ruin this time with her grandma, so I will tell her later.

I head out to my workshop and stare at the dollhouse I'm working on. It's a pretty basic build frame wise, but it's the details and painting that will take up the time. It's why I can't seem to get my head in the game to work today.

I decide to set the dollhouse aside and work on a simple birdhouse to be sent to consignment. I'll do the painting later.

I can build these birdhouses in my sleep, so while I work my mind is elsewhere. I think of Lilly and Sage with the horse and know I need to call Ella later. This news will hit her hard, and she's been more emotional, since getting pregnant.

I also decide it's time to hire a ranch hand to help out and keep an eye on our horses. It's also time I looked at bringing in a few boarders. There's an apartment above the barn, and it even has a small kitchen, which will be perfect for a single guy. With the job, comes room and board, making hiring someone easier.

I pull out my phone and text Mac. He said he knew a guy from his reservation that was looking for some ranch hand work and a place to stay. Not everyone in the area will hire people from the reservation, but Jason's family has always been friends with them with Mac being from the reservation and adopted into Jason's family.

He shoots me the guy's phone number. His name is Dakota, which Mac told me means friend.

The conversation is short. He's excited to find work and help his parents out. Mac mentioned his dad was diagnosed with cancer. The treatment bills are adding up, and he hasn't been able to work. His mom picked up a job, and the tribe helps too, but they are barely getting by. If I'm being honest, his story touched me, and I wanted to help out, so it's perfect timing.

He will be here tomorrow to get settled. I want him to get to know the place before we bring in some horses to board. Sage has a few people on her waiting list, who are looking for a place to board. She said she'd talk to them for me.

So, in a few days, once everything calms down, and Dakota is settled, I'll reach out to her.

I go back inside, figuring I will go join my wife and her grandma. I've spent enough time away from her today when I hear her phone ring.

I thought she took it outside with her, but I find it on her nightstand. I grab it, intending to take it out with me, but I freeze in my tracks when I see the name.

Liam.

Why is her ex calling? Have they been talking? What the hell could he possibly want now?

I stop and take a deep breath. If I want her to trust me, I have to be willing to trust her in return. But for the first time, I'm starting to feel a bit of what she might be feeling with me, and I don't like it one damn bit.

The phone stops ringing, but I don't move. How can she fix how I'm feeling? If I can nail that down, then maybe, I can figure out how to get her to open up to me.

My mind blanks, because if I'm honest, I'm pissed and hurt. I walk outside to the garden and pause when I hear Anna Mae's laugh. I have to believe it's not her fault he's calling. She wasn't expecting him to call, or she'd have taken her phone with her.

I walk over to her, and when she looks up, the smile falls off her face.

"Everything okay?" She asks.

I hand her the phone.

"Your phone rang. Figured I'd bring it out to you." I say and manage to keep my voice steady.

Then, I turn around and walk right back inside.

Chapter 15

Grandma is filling me in on some wild Las Vegas stories I apparently missed out on, and I'm pretty sure she's made them up. There's no way five different guys asked her to marry them that weekend.

"I'm telling you I should have accepted that George guy, his suit was expensive. I bet I'd make a good sugar baby, don't you think?" Grandma says.

I swear some days I can't believe the words that come out of her mouth. She's the perfect distraction I needed today. I've been in a weird place of self-doubt since Dallas.

"Grandma! You couldn't be a sugar baby!" I say in a fake shocked voice.

She narrows her eyes at me "Why the hell not?" She asks.

"Because your boobs are real!" I bust out laughing, and so does she.

It's then that Royce comes out, and he's not his smiling self. Instead of the soft warm eyes I'm used to, his whole face is stone cold. I know things haven't been right between us, but this is way off base. Something is wrong.

"Everything okay?" I ask.

Without a word, he hands me my phone.

"Your phone rang. Figured I'd bring it out to you." He says, his voice flat and cold.

Before I can even say a word, he turns and walks back into the house. What the hell just happened? I sit there shocked. I've never seen this icy side of Royce before, and I have to say I'm not a fan of it, not one bit.

"What was all that about?" Grandma asks.

"I have no idea," I say, still staring after him.

Finally, I realize it must have been something with my phone that upset him. I can't think of anything he would have found on there other than a few photos I took, while he was working. I open my phone and pull up my missed call.

"Oh, shit," I say out loud.

"What is it, girl? Don't keep me waiting."

"Liam called," I say.

"What the hell does that cheating bastard want?"

"I don't know. He's called a few times, but I never answered. He's left some voice mails saying he needs to talk to me, but I have no interest in talking to him."

"Why are you telling me this?" Grandma asks.

"What do you mean? You asked."

"Yes, but you need to be telling your husband. He's been working his hot, sexy ass off to prove to you he's not Liam, and bam, there's Liam on your phone, and you haven't told him. How quickly the tables flip." She shakes her head.

"What are you talking about?"

"Now, he's worried you will want to run back to that creep. He's nervous you're keeping stuff from him."

"No way in hell I want to go back to Liam," I say, almost disgusted.

"You sure about that? You have an amazing, hot, and sweet guy begging to be let in, but you use Liam as an excuse to keep him out. I saw what he did to you firsthand, and even I wonder sometimes." She stands up, shaking her head. "I'm going to go. You two need to talk."

Before she walks out of the garden gate, she turns back to me. "You do need to see what

Liam wants before he shows up here, but you need to talk to Royce first."

She's right. I need to set this straight. If Grandma is even close to guessing how Royce is feeling, then I need to fix it.

I stand up and dust myself off, before heading inside. I make us a couple of glasses of sweet tea and then go in search of my husband. I find Royce in his workshop, sanding a piece of wood.

"Jason was here. Another horse was dropped off at the church, and they don't think he's going to make it. Two horses were also stolen last night closer to the interstate, so I called Dakota. He'll be here tomorrow to get settled in, and then I'll talk to Sage about boarding some horses." He says without even turning to face me, and his voice is as flat as it was out in the garden.

We had talked about hiring Dakota the other day and starting to board horses. We liked the idea of having someone in the barn, especially at night with everything going on. Plus, to help with the animals and for the additional income.

I set the iced tea on the workbench next to him and place my hand on his arm. "Can we talk?" I ask in a soft voice.

He sighs and puts the sandpaper down, turning towards me. Picking up the tea, he leans against his workbench, crosses one leg over the other, and looks at me. Finally, the cold look is gone, but I'm not sure I like the look that has replaced it any better. He looks unsure and almost scared.

"That isn't the first time Liam has called. It started shortly after we married. I sent them all to voice mail. I haven't answered a single one. He has left two voice mails both saying he needs to talk to me and asking me to call him back, but I haven't. I thought he'd have gotten the hint to stop by now."

"You don't know what he wants?" He asks.

"No, and really, I don't care. I don't want to talk to him or have anything to do with him."

Royce sets his glass down and walks over to me, placing his hands on my waist.

"Why don't you call him and find out what he wants, and get it over with." He suggests.

I just shake my head. "I'm not ready. He ruins everything, and things with us have been better than I ever could have hoped for. I'm scared it will spoil everything." I whisper the last part.

It's like watching a wall drop, and my sweet husband is back.

"You aren't alone. I will be right here by your side when you're ready."

"I promise to let you know when I'm ready to call, and you'll be right here and hear it all, okay?"

"Deal." He leans in and gently kisses me, but I pull away before he can deepen it. His eyes find mine full of questions.

"I want to know what was on your mind when you brought the phone out to me."

His eyes flick over my face before he turns to look off to the side of the room.

"At first, I realized how you must have felt, after the Dallas trip, and I hate that you felt that way. Then, I don't know. All the doubts filled me that maybe you had been talking to him and not telling me."

I wrap my arms around his neck.

"I know what it's like to be on the receiving end of that, Royce, and I won't ever do that to anyone, much less you." I kiss his jaw. "My sweet." I kiss the corner of his mouth. "Sexy." I kiss the other corner of his mouth. Then, I move my lips over his, whispering against them. "Perfect husband."

His whole body shutters, as his grip on me tightens, and he lifts and spins me to sit on his workbench.

"I'm sorry, my sweet girl. I should have trusted you. It's not fair to ask you to put your trust in me, but then, not give you mine in return." His voice is hoarse, as he steps between my legs, and I can feel how hard he is.

"We aren't perfect, Royce, and we'll have moments like this. But being able to sit here and talk to you and hash this out, means so much more to me than I will ever be able to tell you."

Then I kiss him. I kiss him because I think I will die if I don't. Because I don't know how else to explain how I feel; there just aren't the words. He kisses me back with just as much intensity, while his hands roam my body.

I reach down and pull his shirt over his head, only breaking our kiss for a moment. His lips are back on mine, as he pulls off my shirt and then starts placing lazy kisses on my neck while unhooking my bra.

His lips travel to the stiff peaks of my nipples, as his hands unbutton and unzip my pants, but he doesn't move me to take them off. He just continues to make love to each nipple, before kissing his way down to my belly button.

"Lift up." He whispers, sliding my pants and underwear down, and then falls to his knees in front of me.

He doesn't tease, he just dives in with his tongue on my pussy, like a starved man. He's quickly learned how to play my body, like his own personal instrument, and he does it well. Within minutes, I can't stop the orgasm that crashes into me. My thighs lock around his head, and he doesn't stop, until I all but collapse backwards on the bench.

He removes his pants, as he stands up and takes his spot between my legs. He wraps his arms around my hips, pulling me right to the edge of the workbench. I put my arms around his neck, and he watches my face, as he slowly enters me. This has become one of his favorite things to do, watch me, while he's inside of me.

I try to tell him with my eyes how much he means to me, how I won't do anything to mess this up, and how much I need him. Everything I can't say with words right now.

He slides in and out of me nice and slow, never breaking eye contact.

"You feel so good, my sweet girl." He whispers, kissing me and quickening his pace. He angles his hips to hit just the right spot inside me. And when he hits that perfect spot over and over again, it's as if he's telling me how much he loves me.

As he runs his teeth over that spot on my neck that drives me crazy, it's the tipping point, and my climax crashes into me, and all I can do is hold on to my husband. I'm just starting to relax, when a few more thrusts send Royce over the edge as well, feeling his hot cum inside me, sets off another mini orgasm that has me gasping for air.

"I think this might be my new favorite way to end my workday." Royce chuckles into my neck, once we have caught our breath. He picks up our clothes and puts them in my lap. Before I can comment, he's sweeping me into his arms and to our room for round two.

Chapter 16

I got up early this morning to finish up the order I was working on. I wanted to make sure I got it done on time, but still had time to spend with my wife today, since it's her day off. It took a little longer than I expected. I rush into the house ready to apologize for being late for our breakfast, only to find the house quiet and still.

I make quick work of checking the kitchen and living room before I peek out front. Her car is still here, so I head to the bedroom. Is she still sleeping? I don't care if she is. It's her day off, and if she needs the rest, I'm more than happy to pamper her. I just want to make sure she's okay.

What I find breaks my heart. My wife is curled up in bed with a heating pad on her lower belly with pain on her face. I gently sit down on the edge of the bed, where she's facing me, and touch her arm.

"What's wrong, my sweet girl?" I ask.

"I'll be fine." She whispers, and I know she doesn't want me to worry and fuss over her, but it's too late. I am worried, and I will fuss over her. It's my privilege to do so, as her husband.

"Damn right, you'll be fine, but that's not what I asked you." I keep my voice soft, and when her eyes meet mine, I see the war of whether to tell me or not. Thankfully, the truth wins out. She breaks eye contact, and it feels like a cloud covering the sun on my skin.

"Just got my period, and it's bad. The heat will help, and I should be better tomorrow."

"What do you need?" I ask her.

"For you to leave me alone for a bit." She snaps at me, but I don't even flinch. I have two younger sisters, who would get snappy, during their time of the month, too. The only difference is Mom would take care of them, and Dad and I just stayed out of their way. It was this time of the month we normally tackled any projects that needed to be done outside of the house.

I rub her arm, step out to the living room, and call my sister, Maggie. She got her periods the worst, so I know she will know what to do.

"Hey, big brother!" She greets me.

"Maggie, I need some help. Anna Mae got her period, and she's having bad cramps like you used, too. How can I help?"

"Ahhh, poor thing. Make sure she's taking ibuprofen as directed day and night for the next forty-eight hours at least. When she's lying down on her side, rub her lower back. Cuddle with her and watch TV, even if she tries to force you away. Once she's sitting up, get her some coffee, chocolate, and some of her favorite foods. Whatever she's craving. Offer to go buy her pads or tampons. Most importantly, don't let her push you away, okay?"

"Good, lord. No wonder Dad had me hide out in the workshop every month." I shake my head.

"Yeah, it was really bad, when Ella and I got it at the same time. Sometimes, we wanted to be together, and other times, we couldn't stand each other's voices. It's hit or miss. Oh, one more thing."

"Yeah?" I ask.

"If she has bad ones like this several times in a row, make sure to have her go see her doctor. They can give her some medication that will help. That's what they did for me."

"Thanks, Maggie."

"No problem, big brother. If she craves something, let us know. Nick would be happy to cook it and bring it over." She says.

"Always!" I hear Nick yell in the background.

"You guys doing good?" I ask her. I hate that it's been a week since we talked last.

"Yes, everything is on track for the wedding at the end of the summer. Though, I'm wishing we had hit the chapel with you and Anna Mae in Las Vegas when we had the chance."

We both laugh and say goodbye. I know Anna Mae has some chocolate in the cabinet, so I go grab it, before heading back into the room.

"Hey, baby. Have you taken any medicine?" I ask softly.

"No." She says, her voice flat.

I nod and go back to the kitchen, grabbing some water and the ibuprofen, like Maggie suggested.

"Can you sit up and take these?" I ask.

She sighs but sits up, takes the medicine, and grabs the chocolate I set on the nightstand earlier.

"Want anything to eat?" I ask.

She shakes her head and settles back on her side on the heating pad.

"Do you have what you need, or do you need me to run to the store?" I ask.

"I have what I need." She says, her voice now soft.

I take off my shoes and my jeans and crawl into bed gently behind her. I turn the TV on and pull up the reality show she likes that's on the DVR, and I press my chest to her back, giving her my warmth.

"You don't have to lay here with me." She says.

"I know I don't, but I'm going, too."

"I'm sure you have better things to do." She says.

"There's nothing more important than being here for my wife. I love you, my sweet Anna Mae, and I would take this pain from you if I could. Since I can't, I'm going to sit here and watch this awesome show with you. The second you need anything, I'm going to be here to get it for you, so stop fighting it." I rub her arm.

I see the hint of a smile on her face before she turns to watch TV. She knows I'm not a fan of this show, but I will watch it with her all day if it makes her feel better.

About fifteen minutes into the second show, her steady breathing tells me she's asleep. At least, she was able to get comfortable. I lay there for a bit, enjoying her back pressed against me. I check my phone while staying quiet not to wake her.

Ella: I'm making chocolate muffins for Anna Mae, and I'll leave them on your porch, so I don't bother her.

I carefully get out of bed, making sure I don't wake her, and go out to the porch and find the bag with a few tins of muffins in them. I take them to the kitchen and find what I need to make tacos. I know they are Anna Mae's favorite, and I hope she will want them for dinner.

I then head back to the bedroom and find her still asleep. One of my favorite things to do is watch her sleep. Not in a creepy way, but this is the one time all her walls are down.

I crawl back into bed, as she starts to stir.

"Hey, beautiful. Ella dropped off some chocolate muffins. Do you want one?" I ask.

"Yes, please." She says, and she pulls herself up.

I go to the kitchen and get her the muffins and some water, while she wakes up. She seems to be feeling better after her nap, and I hope that holds. I make note of the time, and it's still three more hours until she can have more medicine, so I set an alarm on my phone. Maggie said it was important to keep the ibuprofen in her for the first day or two, and I trust her.

I bring the plate and water into the bedroom just as Anna Mae is getting settled back into bed. She takes a large bite of the muffin and groans.

"These are so good. Ella is amazing. I need to get her into the shop, so I can pamper her, as a thank you." She says.

"You feeling better? You look better." I ask.

"Yeah, I think the meds kicked in."

"Good, I set my alarm, so I'll know when you're ready for the next dose."

Her eyes go soft, as she looks at me. Setting the plate down, she reaches for me. I go willingly, as she pulls me in for a kiss.

A short, sweet, soft kiss that ends entirely too soon.

"Thank you for taking care of me." She whispers.

"There's nowhere I'd rather be. Want to watch some more TV?"

"Yes, but let's rent that action movie you wanted to see."

I didn't think she wanted to see that one, so I'm a bit shocked.

"We can watch one of your movies." I offer.

She shrugs, "I'd rather watch that one."

I shake my head and pull it up. We cuddle together in bed, and it's the perfect evening.

I hate she's not feeling good, but being able to hold her and just snuggle isn't something I would pass up for the world.

Chapter 17

It's been a great almost two weeks since Anna Mae let me take care of her. We stayed in the cocoon of our room all day; talked between watching TV. Since then, things have been perfect with us. She accepts me taking care of her, and her walls are down. We have talked about anything and everything from our childhoods, family, friends, school, and more.

Dakota got here and settled in. He took right to the job and is talented with the animals. When Anna Mae asked about getting some chickens, he jumped on board. His mom raised chickens, so he was able to help us set everything up, and even take care of them too, though it's not in his job description.

A few days ago, we took on our first boarder. A city family who has a country home here for the weekends. They don't want to keep animals and staff on the property, so they were on Sage's waitlist. When she talked us up, they met us and loved the barn. When Dakota and their son seemed to connect, and he agreed to give their son riding lessons, they were hooked.

With Dakota running things so well, I have loved finding out the small things about my wife. Things like she stands on her tiptoes when she washes her face in the mirror, and she loves it when I walk up behind her and press my body into hers. When I wrap my arms around her waist and pull her in, her ass fits perfectly against my cock.

Things like she closes her eyes when she takes that first sip of coffee each morning and savors it, before drinking the rest. When she's reading, she stops and stretches her neck from side to side, before starting each chapter. She's most at ease with me, when we're drinking coffee on the porch in the early morning.

She likes to curl up on the corner of the couch under a blanket to read like she is now, and I'm sitting in a chair next to her, pretending to read, but I can't concentrate on a single word in front of me. All I want to do is sneak glances at her.

When there's a knock on the door, we both look at the door, like it's going to reveal who is there.

"You expecting anyone?" She asks.

"Nope," I say, as I get up to get the door.

The man I find on our front porch isn't one I've seen before. He takes me in as I do him before he asks, "Is Anna Mae here?"

I hesitate, wanting to protect her. Who is this guy? I can't be too careful with everything going on in town lately. But when Anna Mae sees him from behind me, she pushes me out of the way and throws herself into his arms. A surge of jealousy runs through me.

She squeals, as he picks her up and swings her around.

Jealousy, like I've never known I was capable of feeling floods me. I should be the only guy putting a smile that big on her face. I should be the only guy with his arms wrapped around her curvy body. I should be the only guy she presses her breasts to like that. Not him. Not this guy who looks like he just blew in from the city.

A city like Dallas. A sense of dread rushes over me, as he sets her down, and they look at each other with huge smiles. This isn't her ex, right? She wouldn't be happy to see him, right?

When she looks back at me, her face drops. I can only imagine what she sees on mine. I don't try to hide it. She reaches over and takes my hand.

"Royce, this is my brother, Jesse. Jesse, this is my husband, Royce." She says, and instantly, all the feelings vanish at the word brother.

I laugh at myself and offer him my hand.

"Hey, come on in." I shake his hand and sweep my arm behind me to the open door.

"I heard you got married in Las Vegas and had to come to see for myself," Jesse says, as we sit in the living room.

"Let me guess. Grandma called spinning her wild tales?" Anna Mae says.

"Oh, yes. Apparently, she had eight marriage proposals." He laughs.

"Oh, she told me it was only five." Ann Mae chuckles. "How's your wife doing?"

Instantly Jesse's face goes cloudy, as he shrugs and changes the subject.

"Oh, no. I want to hear about this wedding! If you had called, I'd have been out there by your side first flight out." Jesse says.

"I know, but it wasn't planned. We kind of woke up married. Neither of us remembers it."

She cringes.

Jesse's eyes shoot to me. I'm sitting beside Anna Mae with my arm over the couch behind her.

"I had been trying for almost a year now to get her to even go on a date with me. I knew about her ex and the basics, so I just kept trying. When she wanted out of the marriage, I wouldn't let her. I think it has worked out." I smile at her, and she smiles back at me.

"It has. How long are you in town?" She asks him.

"Few days. Was going to go stay with Grandma." He says.

"You'll stay with us," I say, earning me a blinding smile from my wife, so I continue. "You're always welcome here no notice needed."

I haven't met my wife's family outside of her grandma, so I'm happy he's here.

We get him settled in the guest room, and I leave him and Anna Mae to talk, while I start dinner. I'm glad her brother came to visit, but I'm a bit shocked her parents haven't. They only live a few hours away, whereas Jesse is on the other side of the country. I know she isn't close to them, so I don't push the issue.

Maybe, I can ask Mrs. Willow next time I see her.

At dinner, the conversation is light, talking about childhood memories and fun times. It's great to get another look into Anna Mae's childhood. We have some wine on the back porch after dinner, and that's when Jesse opens up.

"Sofie has been cheating on me." He says of his wife.

Anna Mae gasps, "Oh, Jesse, I'm so sorry."

"She knows I know, and we both pretend I don't, and that it's not happening." He says, looking into his wine glass.

I watch Anna Mae take his hand. "I love you, Jesse, and no one knows better than me how much the one person who promised to love you forever who then goes and cheats on you can kill your soul. I know it's not easy, but you need to do this for yourself. She's shown she doesn't care about you and your feelings, so stop thinking of her and think of you."

"We've built this whole life together. We share everything. Friends, our home, and even work at the same place. I lose it all if I leave because no one is going to care about me. I'll look like the bad guy for leaving her. I saw it happen with a coworker." Jesse sounds defeated.

"You're always welcome here. Ranch work may not be your thing, but I know some people who could use some extra hands, during the selling season this summer. I'm sure you could find a job in Dallas if you want to move back to the city." I tell him.

His eyes shoot to mine. "You mean that?"

"Of course, you're family. The only family other than your grandma, who has cared to make sure she's okay, after a Las Vegas wedding. Who knows what kind of creep I could have been." I tell him.

The corner of his mouth curves up into a grin.

I continue, "Besides, Anna Mae told me, when she was in the same situation you offered for her to come stay with you. You gave her an out, and while I didn't know her then, I'm grateful you did."

"Thank you. I need to make some plans and get things in place before I even file paperwork, so I'll let you know." He nods.

The rest of the night the conversation stays light, and it's good just to be with family.

· · · ● ● · ● ● · · ·

The next day we invited my family over, along with Mrs. Willow to have dinner. With all ten of us in the house, it's the most people we have had here at once, and Anna Mae is loving every minute of it.

Jason is fussing over Ella, making sure she's sitting down and relaxing. My mom is sitting right next to her, and my dad is sitting right beside my mom. Nick is in the kitchen and has pretty much taken over cooking for us, and Maggie is right by his side.

Jesse, Mrs. Willow, Anna Mae, and I are at the dining room table talking when Anna Mae's phone rings. She sends it to voice mail, but not before Jesse notices.

"Why is Liam calling you?" He asks.

The house goes quiet, and all eyes turn to Anna Mae. I put my hand on her thigh to remind her she isn't alone, and I'm right here for her. I don't like him calling her, but I'm not going to push her into something she isn't ready for either. To be honest, I don't think I'm ready for it myself.

She sighs, "I honestly don't know. I just send him to voice mail. I haven't answered, and all he says if he leaves a message is he needs to talk to me and for me to call him back. I don't want to talk to him, but part of me wonders if it's important somehow, though I'm not sure how."

"I told her she just needs to find out what he wants, then tell him to go to hell." Mrs. Willow huffs.

"I agree with you on that one," I say to Mrs. Willow, as she nods in approval at me.

"I have to agree here. Find out what he wants, and then tell him to leave you alone." Jesse agrees.

"I know. Things are going so well, and he ruins everything. I just wanted to hold on to this a bit longer. I promise soon that I will. Not now, and not with everyone here having a good time." She says.

Everyone seems to agree, and slowly, the conversations all start up again.

I lean in and whisper in her ear, "Every person in this room is on your side, sweet girl, whenever you're ready." I kiss her temple, before sitting back.

The rest of the night is filled with lots of laughs, stories, and new memories we're making.

This right here is the perfect night. Too bad perfect never lasts long, right?

Chapter 18

My brother is heading home today, and he won't let me drive him to the airport. He rented a car when he got here, and he wants the time to think on the drive back into Dallas. I get that. There's a lot to sort out, and no one knows that better than me.

We are standing in the living room, and Royce says his goodbyes, before turning to me. "I'll be in my workshop if you need me." He says, leaning in to kiss my cheek, before giving my brother and me some time to say goodbye ourselves.

"Walk me out?" Jesse asks, slinging his arm over my shoulder.

"I like him, and you know I didn't like Liam. I didn't like how he treated you most of all, but you seemed happy, so I let it be. But Royce?" He stops for a moment, "Royce worships you. He's always watching and making sure you're okay, and he seems to know what you need before you do. Always there with water, coffee, food, or whatever it was. I've also never seen you this happy."

My eyes mist over. "Thanks, Jesse. I don't remember a time that I've been this happy."

He nods, pulling me in for a hug. "Call Liam and see what he wants and get it over with, so you can move on with this incredible life here. Don't let him screw this up, too."

"I promise I won't. Also, move back out here. If not with me, with Grandma. I miss you so much, and I could use having you back here."

"Maybe, once all this is over. I've been thinking of coming home, too. Thankfully, there are no kids involved, or this would be ugly."

"No kidding. I said the same thing when I was going through my divorce." I agree.

A few more hugs and I love yous are exchanged before he finally drives away.

I walk up to the house and sit on the front porch to think. I know what Jesse said is true. I need to get this thing with Liam out of the way. Letting it hang over our heads, I can't expect to have any kind of life with Royce.

I'm picturing the life in front of us here on the ranch, kids in the yard, family get togethers, and it hits me on the head, like ice falling from the roof.

Am I in love with my husband?

No, I can't be. I care for him, sure, but I've kept my heart guarded for a reason. There's no way I can be in love with him. I know he loves me. He says it daily now, and I feel strongly for him. I can't imagine a life without him, and I don't want to.

I realize I want to love him. I want him to be the person to which I finally let my defenses down. But I can't do that with Liam lurking around, or with what he wants being unknown.

This steals my resolve. I'm going to end this now.

I make my way through the house and out to Royce's workshop. As soon as he hears the door close, he sets down what he's working on and turns to face me.

"He get off okay?" He asks about my brother.

"Yes. Royce?"

"Yeah, sweet girl?" He asks his eyes on me.

"I think I'm ready to call Liam and get it over with. I don't want this hanging over us anymore."

He nods, but I see the tension in his smile. He holds out his arms, and I walk right into them. Leaning against his workbench, he turns me to rest my back to his chest and wraps his arms around my waist, kissing my temple.

"I'm here." He whispers in my ear.

I nod, take a deep breath, and pull up Liam's number. I stare at it for a minute, wanting to resolve this, and dreading it at the same time. Finally, I hit call and flip it to speakerphone. No secrets between me and Royce.

"Anna Mae?" He answers, shock in his voice. Every muscle in my body fills with tension, and I know Royce feels it because he starts nuzzling my neck, pulling me tighter to him.

"Yes. What do you want, Liam?" I keep my tone flat and cold.

"Damn, I can't believe you called me back." I know that tone in his voice, and I know he has a slight smile on his face. I hate it.

"Is there a reason for your calls, or were they just to harass me?"

"No." He clears his throat. "Listen, I sold the condo, and as I was packing up, I found some of your stuff. A few things I think you'll want, photos and all. I also need to talk to you in person."

"No. You can mail my stuff to my grandma's. I'll reimburse your shipping, but whatever you have to say, tell me now, and let's get this over with. I have a life, Liam, and you aren't a part of it anymore, by your choice."

"Listen, this isn't me just wanting to bull shit for old time's sake. This is serious. Can we please meet and talk soon?" I know Liam. I was with him for years, and with the tone he's using, there's something in there. He sounds... scared, and a little desperate, maybe?

My mind starts to race, trying to figure out what it could be before I realize this is my chance to have closure. Get it done, so I can start this life with Royce and give myself to him completely. Maybe, I need this more than I thought.

"Fine, I'll check with the salon and text you a day. Make it work, or the answer is no." I tell him.

"I promise any day or time I'll be there, just let me know when."

"Goodbye, Liam." I hang up before he can get another word in.

"You know I'm coming with you, right?" Royce says, and I know from his tone he's clearly unhappy I even agreed to go.

I turn in his arms, knowing he isn't going to like what comes next. I run my hands up his chest and wrap them around his neck.

"I need to do this on my own," I say. He opens his mouth to argue, and I place a finger over it. "You being there will cause drama. I know Liam, and I don't want that. I figure I have three days coming up. I can head to Dallas after work, get a hotel room, and check out that salon I wanted to check out. The one I told you about the other day. Meet Liam early the next day, and then come home. I will tell you everything, and then spend the rest of my time off in bed with my sexy husband."

I see the battle in his eyes. The battle of wanting to protect me and wanting to give me what I want.

"Let me do this, Royce," I whisper. "Let me put this behind us once and for all. I didn't realize I needed this closure. Let me do this for us."

The defeat I see on his face breaks my heart. He just nods and doesn't say a word.

The next few days, before I leave for Dallas are filled with tension. He tries to act like nothing is wrong and fails miserably. Word gets around, and all the girls call me at some point, mostly telling me I'm crazy. His sisters seem a little mad while asking me what I was thinking.

I'm standing in our room packing my jeans and t-shirt in an overnight bag, when Royce enters, standing in the doorway watching.

Our eyes lock, and no words are spoken, as he stalks over to me, and his mouth crashes down on mine. He isn't gentle, and it's exactly what I need right now. He starts removing my clothes and his. The fire in his eyes shows me he needs this just as much as I do.

Still, with deafening silence, he picks me up and tosses me on the bed. He moves over me, and I know my gentle husband has been taken over by the side of him that needs to claim me, making me remember I'm his.

He settles between my thighs, pushing my legs wide, and in one solid thrust, he slams into me, causing us to moan. Not giving me time to adjust, he starts thrusting in and out in a hard punishing rhythm. I reach up and brace myself against the headboard, so my head doesn't hit it. A brief nod of approval comes from Royce before he slams his mouth back down on mine.

His kiss is just as brutal as his thrusts are, and the moment he pulls back from the kiss he pulls out of me, too. I whimper at the loss of connection, but he's flipping me over. He pushes my shoulders down into the bed, so my ass is up in the air.

His strong, rough hands grip my hips, and he slams back into me. This time I can't hold it in. "Royce!" I scream his name.

"When you are in Dallas, I want you to feel me between your thighs and know that... You. Are. Mine." He grunts with each thrust. This is a side I haven't seen from Royce before. Hard and claiming, and I love it. I needed this; the reality of it, after the last few days.

"I want you walking funny, so he knows you've been claimed." He slams into me even harder, and the pain turns to pleasure, as one of his hands follows the curve of my hips, before finding my clit and rubbing rough circles on it.

I push my ass further into him. "That's right, baby. Give me my pussy. MINE!" In the next moment, his hand leaves my hips and slaps my ass. The searing pain lasts only a minute, and holy hell, I've never been so turned on. It must have registered what he did because he freezes.

"Fuck, don't stop!" I beg.

His thrusts start up again just as brutal, and my climax builds. He slaps me again, before gripping my hips to control the pace.

"You like that, my wife?"

I can't form words, so I nod my head.

"Seems my sweet girl has a dirty side to her. I fucking love it." He says, leaning over my body and whispering in my ear.

My climax is so close. Just a few more strokes and I know I'll be there. He must feel it too because he pulls out completely.

"No!" I whine, and he chuckles. He turns me on the bed to face the other wall, keeping my ass up, and thrusts back into me from behind.

"Think I can't tell, when you are about to cum? I know everything about your body. Every noise and spot that drives you crazy." I grunt, as he runs his hands up my back and grabs my shoulders, pulling me up on my knees on the bed. My back is to his chest, and he's still pounding in and out of me.

One arm goes around my chest and starts playing with my nipples, and the other finds my clit and starts rubbing it at such a punishing pace that it steals my breath.

"Open your eyes, my dirty girl." He whispers in my ear. When my eyes snap open, the sight in front of me causes my pussy to tighten, and my climax washes over me.

We are right in front of the mirror on my dresser, and it's the most erotic thing I've ever seen. Me, on full display, with Royce thrusting in and out of me while playing with me.

I throw my head back on his shoulder and let another orgasm take over. My whole body shakes, and I feel like I'm falling at the same time his arms are holding me in place.

"That's right. Strangle your husband's cock." He grunts into my ear right before he releases into me. The pulsing of his hot cum causes another small orgasm to overtake me before we both collapse on the bed.

"Fuck, I love you," Royce says, pulling me in for a gentler kiss. I've never heard him cuss this much in my life, but I have to admit it's a turn on.

I don't think he gets much sleep that night, because every time I drift off, he's waking me up again either by thrusting into me or with his mouth, eating me to an orgasm.

If his plan is to make my whole body like jello, so I can't go to Dallas, I think he might be well on his way.

Chapter 19

Anna Mae: Leaving work now. Text you, when I get to Dallas.

That's the text I just got, and it doesn't calm my nerves one bit. I can't concentrate, and I have been wanting to punch my hand through a wall all day, but I know she wouldn't like to come back to seeing holes everywhere.

If she comes back at all.

The voice in the back of my head has been whispering stuff like that all day. Last night, I don't know what got into me. Taking her so roughly like that, but she has never been so wet or cum so hard, so I know she loved it. She seemed to need it as much as I did. I wanted to remind her and me that she's mine. I needed to give her a reminder of what she was coming home to.

If she comes back at all.

The voice is getting louder and louder, and I can't take it. She left for Dallas. Part of me was hoping she'd changed her mind at work today and decided to come home to me. I'm terrified that whatever he has to say will change her mind about us, and that he will talk her into another chance.

I can't sit here waiting, so I head to our room and seeing the bed, memories from last night flash into my head. A vice grips my heart, and I send up a silent prayer.

Please, Lord, don't let that be the last time I get to be inside my wife.

It almost doesn't seem like something I should be talking to the Lord about, but it's the most honest and raw I can be right now.

A knock on the door pulls me from my thoughts, and I open the door to find Jason there.

"Go away," I tell him, knowing he knows what's going on.

"Pack a bag. I'm not going to let you sit here and climb the walls overthinking things. Nick has a hunting cabin a few hours from here, and we're going there for the night, and you'll be back tomorrow."

Getting away for the night sounds perfect, and I remember Nick mentioning the cabin.

There's no cell phone reception there, and I hesitate for only a moment before I quickly pack a bag.

I scribble a quick note to Anna Mae on the off chance she gets home before I do.

I send Dakota a text letting him know I'll be away overnight, but I know he can handle it. Then, we are in my truck, heading for the interstate without a second thought. Ella dropped Jason off, so he could ride with me, but I'm thankful he's letting me drive, so I can work out my thoughts.

On the drive, I know I need to get my head on straight. This is the do or die moment for Anna Mae and me. I feel it in my bones. If she can't put this behind her and finally open up to me, I have to find a way to be okay with no more than what we have now.

I love her, and there's no way I can walk away from her, but I know I will always want more. I will want all of her, and it's going to slowly kill me if I can't have it.

The miles roll by along with the flat north Texas landscape. There's a very minimal amount of traffic on the road, and I almost wish there was a lot more, so my mind wouldn't be able to wander as easily.

As we near a town, Jason suggests we stop and get some groceries and fishing supplies since it's the last town before we reach the cabin. Even here, walking the aisle of the grocery store, memories of my wife assault me. Her favorite foods and I even catch a whiff of her shampoo that has me turning around, hoping she followed me here. Of course, she hadn't.

I finish the drive up to the cabin. Leaving town, the road gets narrow, as I drive through the woods. The sun is starting to sink into the sky, and since I don't know these roads, I want to get in, before it's dark.

"Nick says the key is in a hole in a tree trunk just over here," Jason says, flipping on his phone light.

He finds the key right where Nick said it would be. I have to kick up the power, but everything seems to work. So, we unload the car and take a look around.

It's a small two-bedroom cabin. There's a master bedroom with a queen bed, and the second bedroom is set up with three sets of bunk beds. There's a Jack and Jill bathroom between the two bedrooms.

The main living space is one open room with the living room, dining room, and kitchen. In the corner to provide heat, there's a wood stove. All the walls are logs, and the rugs on the wood floors give the place a comfy feel.

"Nice little place, huh?" Jason asks.

"This isn't a hunting cabin. I was thinking of a one-room cabin with a bed in one corner, a small wood stove in another, and an outhouse around the back. This is more like a vacation cabin in the woods."

Jason nods in agreement and takes his stuff to the bunk room, leaving me the master.

I decide to take a hot shower, seeing if it can relax my muscles that have been strung tight with tension ever since this morning.

As soon as the hot water hits me, it starts working, but sadly, it has the opposite effect. As my muscles relax, I start to think about my wife. What if she calls and can't reach me tonight? What if she calls and needs me? I almost jump out of the shower to race back into town and call her; let her know I'm at the cabin when the voice in the back of my head makes itself known again.

What if she calls to tell you she isn't coming home?

That one thought is what scares me out of heading back into town. I'm not ready to hear it; I don't think I ever will be, but I sure as hell am not ready right now.

I warm up the fried chicken and the few sides I grabbed from the grocery store for dinner tonight. I try to not focus on anything to do with Anna Mae. For a while, I'm able to focus on Maggie's wedding, as I eat and go over her plans in my head, but it's not long before that leads me back to our time in Las Vegas.

I switch gears, trying to focus on Ella and her pregnancy, and on being an uncle for the first time. I'm so damn excited for them. Then, it hits me how much I want that with Anna Mae and the very real possibility that I won't get it.

"You have to get out of your head," Jason says over dinner, startling me. I almost forgot he was here.

"Easier said than done."

"I know. Listen, tomorrow we'll go fishing. Being outside will do you good." He says as I nod in agreement.

I only let the darkness consume me after I clean up and climb into bed. Then, my head goes down a rabbit hole of what ifs. Could I live with it if they are having sex right now? If he's making her cum? Can I forgive her and still have a future with her? Can I let her go if she wants to give him another chance?

I know in my heart I won't have a choice, but I also know it will break me in a way I don't think I can come back from.

I bury my head in the pillow and do something I haven't done since I was in elementary school.

I cry myself to sleep.

Chapter 20

I try calling Royce again, and he doesn't pick up. After getting into Dallas last night and checking out the salon, I tried texting and calling him, but I got nothing all night. I hoped I'd wake up to something this morning and again nothing. Then, this morning, before I went to see Liam, I tried again and still nothing.

Needing to know he's okay, I call Ella, hoping she's heard from him, or at least, she can go by and check on him.

"Anna Mae?" She answers.

"Hey, have you heard from Royce?" I ask, skipping the pleasantries.

She doesn't answer right away, before she sighs, "Yes."

"Is he okay? I've been trying to get a hold of him and can't."

"Yeah, he said he needed some time to think. I'm to tell you he's fine and will talk to you soon."

"Okay," I say stunned.

I end the call and get in my car, heading towards the address Liam gave me. I assume it's some bistro outside the city limits because he always liked those places. He never cared for the crowds in the places downtown.

On the way, I keep thinking about Royce. What does he need to think about? There's only one answer I can come up with.

Us.

He needs to think about us. He's been so patient and understanding. Is this what finally pushed him over the edge? God, I hope not. After everything, I can't lose him.

As I get closer, I notice I'm in a kind of nice neighborhood. Maybe, this is a more local place? I keep waiting for a small little strip mall to come up, but it doesn't, and the address leads me to a house.

Liam is parked in the driveway, leaning against his car, and his face grows into a full on smile when he sees me pull in. I instantly notice the contrasts between Liam and Royce. Where Royce is all muscle and thick in all the right places, Liam is lean and thin. Liam is comfortable in a suit, where Royce prefers jeans and a flannel or casual button-up shirt. Royce is tan, as Liam is more pale skin from spending most of his time in the office. To me, Royce's more rugged look is sexier than any suit Liam could pull off.

As I get out of the car, Liam doesn't move to help me, where Royce would have been at my door, before I turned my car off to help me out. I glance at the house, and it's everything I used to want. Nice neighborhood, fancy landscaping, and large enough to host parties, but too large for me to keep on my own without help.

"Anna Mae!" Liam says and finally moves from his car, going to hug me. I put my hand out and stop him from getting much closer.

"What do you want, Liam?"

His face clouds over, and I notice he looks older, and like he hasn't been sleeping.

"I messed up," he says.

"Ya think?" I can't help the sarcastic comment.

He swallows, and his Adam's apple bobs.

"The baby wasn't mine." Is all he says, but I know what he means. His secretary, who I caught him with, wound up pregnant, and they made it a point to tell me the last time I saw them when we were working out the divorce. The reason the divorce went so quickly is he agreed to whatever to get it done because they wanted to get married.

"Well, what did you expect? She knew you were married, and she still went after you. She doesn't care about cheating, so of course, she'd cheat on you." Is all I can say. I can't comfort him for what he did. He has to live with that.

He looks sad, as he nods and stares at his feet. He's always so assertive and has a plan, but this unsure Liam is throwing me completely off kilter. Then, he looks up and back at the house, before he looks at me.

"What do you think of the house? Want to see inside?" He asks.

"It looks just like the house I was always wanting to buy with you, but no, I don't want to see inside. I want to know why I'm here other than to get my stuff."

"I bought it for us." He says.

Shock rolls through me before I can talk again.

"The house?" I ask, needing to clarify.

"Yes. It's the house you always wanted. The one I should have bought you after we got married, instead of making you stay in my condo. I want you back and another chance. I love you. I always have, and I'll do better. I learned my lesson, and I swear this won't happen again. I'll take more time off from work, and we can go out and do things every weekend like you wanted. I'll be home for dinner every night, and no work after dinner, I swear it. Give me another chance to prove I am the man you married."

My mouth drops open, and all I can do is stand there in shock. He waits and doesn't say anything, as I turn to look at the house and take a few steps away from him.

Actions speak louder than words.

That's what Grandma has always told me since I was little, and she has said those words recently, too.

Liam is standing here using words to win me over, but Royce has been showing me with his actions from day one. He doesn't say he will treat me good, he just does it. He was there when I had cramps and dropped everything to take care of me. But the days I was like that, Liam was nowhere to be found. He wouldn't even stop to get me pads or tampons from the store when I asked, but Royce offered.

Royce helps around the house and makes dinner on days I work. He almost always puts his work down, when I'm home, and when he can't, he begs me to join him in the workshop, which almost always leads to sex on his workbench now. I smile at that. Even during sex, Royce always makes sure I cum before him and more than once. With Liam, once we were married, he couldn't care if I did or not, as long as he got his.

Even before Las Vegas, Royce was always at my side, making sure I had what I wanted or needed, that I ate, had water, or whatever it was. He hasn't wavered in who he is.

God, I've been such an idiot. Of course, he needs time to think. Why am I here? Why didn't I let Royce come with me?

Oh God, what have I done?

I turn to face Liam, who has so much hope in his eyes.

"I'm married, Liam. I don't know why it took you this long to figure out what you had, but I don't want someone who doesn't know it when they have it. I love my husband, and he was there to put me back together when you broke me. He was by my side and never gave up, no matter how much I tried to push him away. Now, I want my stuff, so I can get back to him." I stare him down.

Shock registers on his face first, as his eyes trail to my left hand, and he stares at the ring. Then, disappointment crosses his face, as he turns to his car and pulls a box out of the back seat.

"I didn't think..." He trails off, as he looks at the ring on my hand again.

"It's been over a year, Liam. Did you think I'd sit around and wait on you? Once a cheater, always a cheater. I won't be walked on like that. Not when I have a man who has shown me what real unconditional love is." I say, taking the box from him, as I turn and place it in my car.

"I *am* sorry. She just said all the right things, and I believed her, when she said you didn't care, because you let me spend so much time at the office."

I laugh out loud, which seems to startle him.

"I didn't let you do anything. I asked you more times than I can count to spend time with me. To go do things with me. To stay home. After being basically told work was more important than me, I just stopped. I think I knew then, and I was just happy living in denial until it was thrown in my face. For what it's worth, I forgave you. I did it for myself, so I could move on. Goodbye, Liam. Please, don't contact me again. Next time, my husband will deal with you, because I'm done."

With that, I turn, get in my car, and drive away. I stop at a drive-through, before getting on the interstate to grab lunch and try to call Royce again, but it still goes straight to voice mail.

I send up a silent prayer that I'm not too late, as I make my way home. It's on the way that I know I will fight for him and fight for us. It's my turn to carry us because he's been doing it all this time. He believed in us when I didn't, so now, it's my turn to believe in us, when he can't.

My resolve grows with each mile closer to home I get.

When I get home and pull into the house, I don't see his truck, but I still run inside and call his name. It isn't until I see the letter on the dining room table, I realize he isn't here.

Anna Mae,

I want you to know how much I love you. It's that love that's eating at me right now, while you are with your ex. I've been strong for so long, and I kept telling myself you would come around if I just loved you more and loved you harder.

I don't know what happened with Liam, but I have a pretty good idea what he wanted, and I'm not strong enough to hear it right now. I decided to go to a cabin for a bit with Jason. I need to recharge myself. There's no cell service.

I only want you to be happy. Whatever choice you make, I hope it makes you happy.

I love you with everything I am, and I always will.

Royce

By the time I finish reading the letter, tears are freely running down my face. I did that to him because I was so scared and had my walls up. I didn't let him in and did that to him, to us.

I promised myself on the way here that it was my turn to fight for us. That's what I'm going to do. I head to the kitchen and pour a glass of wine and make a game plan.

I know what I need to do, as I pick up the phone. I try one more time to call Royce, and it still goes to voice mail, so I call Ella instead.

"Hello?" She asks hesitantly.

"Have you heard from Royce? He left me a note saying he went to a cabin with Jason."

"Yeah, I guess they are fishing and stuff."

"I know you're Royce's sister, but I'm asking for your help. This was the wake up call I needed, and I plan to do whatever it takes to win him back."

"Oh, thank God. Hang on." She says.

I hear some tapping sounds before she comes back on the line.

"I just sent a text off to Jason. He will get it when he gets service again. Now, what do you need?"

I tell her my plan, and she decides to call the girls and rally the troops to come over and help.

I'm so glad she's willing to help. If she had told me no, I would completely understand, because she would be on Royce's side no matter what, and I love her for that. But the fact that she wants to help me, makes me love her even more.

I smile and get started on some food and put some more wine in the fridge. It's going to be a long night.

Chapter 21

I didn't sleep much last night. I couldn't get my mind off Anna Mae, and anytime I did manage to drift off, my dreams were filled with her with him. I've never seen a picture of Liam, so it was always some faceless guy, but I knew it was him.

I finally pulled myself out of bed and went out to make coffee. I'm making coffee and breakfast like I do every morning, except this morning, I'm not making it for my wife. I'm making it for my brother-in-law, and that's enough to tighten the vice on my heart.

As the smell of coffee and bacon fills the air, Jason comes into the kitchen.

"Morning." He says as he makes himself a cup of coffee. No other words are spoken until I put breakfast on the table, and we sit down to eat.

"Now, I'm going to tell you this, and then I won't bring the subject up the rest of the day unless you bring it up." He watches me, and I finally nod, before he continues. "I will tell you this, you need to go home and talk to her. Trust in her the same way you want her to trust in you. Now pass the bacon."

I pass him the plate of bacon in almost stunned silence. I know Jason's right; I need to trust her.

"I don't think my heart can take it right now. I just need today, and I promise tomorrow, I'll go home and face the music." I say.

"Then, I'm here until tomorrow, too," Jason says. I will admit it's nice not to be alone.

We finish our breakfast talking about the ranch and the work that needs done this summer. We also talk about WJ's and all the new ideas Nick has. He made Nick a partner in the place. It only seemed right, since it was his cooking that put it on the map.

We have all benefited from that because Nick is always having us try new dishes. Maggie always complains she's going to gain twenty pounds, but I know she loves his food as much as he loves feeding her.

After breakfast, we pack up our fishing stuff and make the short hike down to the river. I have to admit this cabin is in a beautiful location, not too far from the river, and I can see it being a great hunting spot later in the summer.

Once we reach the riverside, we set up and start fishing.

"How's Megan and the baby doing?" I ask. Anna Mae and I haven't seen much of them, and Anna Mae says she hasn't even been into work that she's seen.

"They're doing good. Keeping a low profile, which I think is drumming up more excitement in town than they want. Megan hasn't left the ranch, and Hunter only has a handful of times. They're enjoying being parents, and Hunter is enjoying taking care of both of them."

The twinkle in his eye says he knows exactly how that feels.

"It will be you and Ella soon enough. How's she doing?"

"She's incredible. We had an ultrasound the other day, and hearing the baby's heartbeat and seeing it on screen, was just... I don't have words for it. Amazing isn't even strong enough."

I gulp and force down the lump in my throat. I want that more than anything. I can't help feeling any chance I had of that is slipping away faster than I can hold on to it.

"You know not every relationship is perfect," Jason says. "Ella and I have had our struggles. As you know, our childhoods were polar opposites, and some days while we were courting, it felt like the dream of being here with a wife, kids, and all of it was so far out of grasp. I can remember several times growing up finding my dad sleeping in his office because he and my mom fought, but it always worked out."

I let his words sink in. I know what he's trying to say.

"Ever deal with an ex trying to win your girl back?" I ask.

"No, but Sage and Colt had to deal with something like that. You know they fell in love in high school, and Sage panicked, ran off, and traveled. Well, by the time she got back, Colt had been having a casual fling with Kelli, and he broke it off the second Sage got back to town. But Kelli kept trying to win him back, even going as far as to make it look like Colt was cheating on Sage."

"How did they get through it?" I ask. Sage and Colt's dating was before we got here. We met Sage, while she was traveling, but didn't meet the rest of the family, until Sage and Colt's wedding. That's where Jason met Ella and started us all down this path.

"Colt went after her like a bull in a china shop. Didn't give her a chance to put up too many walls. They locked themselves in a cabin on the ranch, and by the next morning, they were fine. Sage and Megan also got some revenge on Kelli, so there was that." Jason chuckles. "It didn't take long for the town to know what Kelli did. She did it right in the middle of WJ's, so that's why she's not well liked. Everyone was rooting for Sage and Colt for years."

Jason recasts his line, before turning to me again.

"The same way everyone is rooting for you and Anna Mae. You two maybe married, but this is still the courtship or dating part of your relationship. There are going to be bumps, and to be honest, you should be glad this one is getting out of the way. I think she needed closure, and she never got it. This could be the final step before she's ready to take the next step with you."

"Or it could be what she has been waiting for, and she chooses to run back to him."

"And you're just going to lie down and let it happen?" He asks.

"I want her to be happy, and if she's going to be happy with him, then yes, I'd let her go."

Jason nods. "Well, hiding out here isn't going to solve anything. If we leave now, we can be back by dinner. Let me help you through this."

He's right. I need to face this, find out what her choice is, and start moving in whatever direction my life takes. This hanging here in limbo hurts too much. I know her choosing to walk away will hurt more, but there's a slight chance she could choose Liam. I'm still hoping she chooses me, and the pain would go away.

I send up another silent prayer, something I've been doing a whole lot more of lately.

"Okay, let's go," I whisper, almost not wanting to say the words, but Jason hears me.

We pack up and head back to the cabin. He tries to take my mind off things by talking about anything and everything in town, but it doesn't help. All I can see is my wife, and with every step closer to the cabin, the dread I'm feeling gets stronger.

I take my time packing up my stuff at the cabin. If Jason notices he doesn't say anything, he just helps me load up my truck.

I turn on the radio, trying to get lost in the music, as the wheels carry me closer to my new normal, whatever it may be.

Chapter 22

Ella's phone rings, and we both jump.

"Oh, it's Jason." She says, before picking up.

"Hey, baby." She answers and then listens for a minute. "Okay, let me check." She pulls the phone away and mutes it.

"Jason said they are heading back and stopped for gas. He wants to know if he should come here or have Royce drop him back at the ranch?"

"Tell him to go to the ranch, because I want Royce alone. You can tell Jason what's going on, but tell him not to tell Royce, please." I say.

Ella nods, and I see the twinkle in her eye, as she steps on to the porch to talk to her husband.

Last night, Ella and the girls came over and have been helping me decorate the house. We made a game plan, and this morning we hit the ground running.

Colt, Hunter, Mac, and Nick spent the morning painting a few rooms for me. The girls and I ran out and hit some thrift stores and got some decorations and some furniture. Then, we split up. Half the girls took the stuff back to the house to get started, and the rest of us headed to the big box store, picking up the rest of what we needed.

We decided to go with a farmhouse feel, because I love the rustic mixed with the old, and it will match Royce's work well. When I got home, I went out to his workshop and found a few wall hangings I had watched him make over the last few weeks and brought them in to hang up in our living room.

Since we always have coffee together in the morning, Ella made us this cute little coffee bar between the dining room and kitchen.

In the living room, we went with blues and grays, since it matches the couch perfectly, and we have some really good memories on that couch.

While in the bedroom, we kept some of the green and brought in more grays. Maggie's photos stayed above the bed, because I love them, but we rearranged them. In the center, we put up this wall hanging I found, and it was perfect. It says *'Better Together'* which is so us. We are better together, and I hate that it took me so long to realize it, and how much I hurt him in the process.

"Okay, Jason says they're about three hours out, so we need to clean up and get out of here," Ella announces.

Nick has been helping me make dinner. I wanted to make the pulled pork BBQ sandwiches Royce loves but had no idea where to start. Since BBQ is Nick's specialty, he jumped right in.

"Whew," Ella says, sitting down on the couch and rubbing her belly.

"How are you feeling?" I ask her.

"Good, just tired. This little one is stealing all my energy for itself!" She laughs.

"I'm really glad you agreed to help me," I say, sitting down next to her.

"Royce has done so much for me. I'd do anything for him. This I know, is going to make him so happy, and I'm excited to be a part of it." She pulls me in for a hug. "Thank you for making him happy. He deserves it, and so do you."

I take a look around, and the place really came together fast. It finally looks like a home; not someplace waiting for a family to settle into.

"Come on, let's get you dressed up," Sarah says, pulling me back in to the bedroom.

Earlier today, the girls raided my closet and found a dress I bought for a cocktail dinner event I never got to wear. It still had the tags on it. They insisted I dress up for Royce and made sure I wore it with some sexy lingerie. I agreed because I want him to know I am all in.

I get dressed, and then they help with my hair and makeup.

"Okay, we have to go. They're thirty minutes out!" Ella says, and they all head out. Nick gives me cooking instructions, but basically, everything is ready and just keeping warm.

Once they are all gone, and I'm alone waiting for Royce, my nerves truly set in. I hope I'm not too late. I hope he isn't coming home to tell me he can't do this anymore. Not that it matters, because I'm ready to fight. Dirty, if I must. I picked up a few fun things on my way home last night. I will tie him to the bed for a few days if I have to and make him see things my way.

The thought gets me so turned on; I debate on whether I need to go take care of myself before he gets here. But when I see his truck turn down the driveway, I know I don't have time. I go stand in the middle of the living room and smooth down my dress. The butterflies in my belly have multiplied and are frantically trying to get out.

I take a few calming breaths, and then go and meet him on the front porch. He stops in his tracks when he sees me, and his eyes run over me from head to toe twice, before he makes eye contact. He looks run down and tired.

My heart breaks knowing I did this to him, and I hope what I have in store tonight is enough to fix it.

He opens his mouth to say something, but then shuts it and takes a deep breath. He looks scared to talk, so it's up to me.

"I missed you," I tell him.

"I missed you, too." He whispers.

"I hated not being able to talk to you. I needed you." I say softly.

Guilt washes over his face. "I'm sorry, I..."

I rush forward and take his hands in mine. "I get it. It took having that meeting with Liam, but I get it." I stop him.

"How did it go?" He asks, barely above a whisper.

"Well, the baby wasn't his, and the secretary had been cheating on him. I laughed when he told me and said what do you expect." I pause, and Royce's eyes meet mine again, and I see a tiny glimmer of hope there.

I want to skip everything and tell him I'm his, but I need to do this right. I have to get it all out, so this isn't between us anymore. Close this door for both of us, if we are going to move on.

"I don't know. It was like something clicked right then. He kept saying he wanted me back, and that he would treat me better, be home more, and he bought this house for me. The house I wanted so bad when we were married, he went and bought it."

That hope in his eyes quickly dies, and he looks down at his feet. I place my finger under his chin and bring his gaze back to me.

"He kept saying he loved me, and I felt... nothing. When you say it, my heart skips a beat, and I can feel it. When he said it, I cringed. Then, I realized something I should have realized a long time ago." I say and wait. I need him to want to know; I need him to ask.

He takes a shaky breath. "What did you realize?" He asks.

I smile then. "That actions are louder than words. So, you know what I told him?"

His eyes search mine, trying to decide if he wants to know the answer. We are still standing on the porch with his hand in mine, and my body wanting him. I want to push him down right here and jump him. So, I take a deep breath and wait. I will do this right no matter what.

"What did you tell him?" He finally asks.

Chapter 23

I'm scared to know what she told him. I'm trying not to get my hopes up, and I'm avoiding looking at her in this sexy as hell dress. That dress makes me want to forget everything and just take her against the wall of the house.

"What did you tell him?" I ask.

"That his words mean nothing because you have shown me with your actions you love me, even when I pushed you away. I told him I was married, and I love my husband more than I ever thought possible."

Did she just say she loved me?

Before I can open my mouth to ask, she takes two steps forward, until her front is pressed against mine, and my cock grows hard, wanting her no matter the outcome.

"I love you, Royce, and I'm so sorry it took me so long to realize it."

I rest my forehead against hers. Holy shit, the words I never thought I'd hear. The words just a few days ago I thought I was okay with never hearing are suddenly something I can't live without.

"Say it again, sweet girl," I whisper against her lips.

"I love you, my husband." She whispers back. Then, she throws her arms around my neck and kisses me.

I waste no time kissing her back. This is a kiss just hours ago I was wondering if I'd ever get to taste again. As I start to trail my lips down her neck, she lets out a gasp.

"Royce, there's more." She barely gets out. My heart sinks just a little, but I know at this moment, even if something happened between them, I'd forgive it if she wants me and this life. I'd forgive her for anything.

"Come inside." She says and takes my hand.

I follow behind her, and from the moment she opens the door, I wonder if we are in the right house.

"You decorated?" I ask.

"Yes, with some help from Maggie, Ella, and Jason's family."

I take in the blue and gray living room. It feels cozy and like a home. She's hung a few of the signs I made on the wall and seeing she wants to display them, gives me pride. Knowing she likes my work, makes it all worth it.

She guides me to the kitchen, and I just take everything in.

"The coffee bar was Ella's idea since we have coffee together every morning." She says with a blinding smile on her face.

I'm so choked up all I can do is nod. She leads me back to our bedroom, which is also redone. The wall above the bed captures my attention. Maggie's photos are still there but, in the center, it says, *Better Together*.

"It's perfect," I say, and her whole face lights up.

"Do you really like it?" She asks.

"I love it because you did it. You made this our home." I choke out the last word.

"I love you so much. No matter how hard I pushed, you were right there demonstrating what real love was. Showing me you would always be there. I'm so sorry it took me this long to realize that, and I'm sorry I hurt you. That was never my intention. I didn't realize how badly I needed to close off that chapter of my life before I could move on with you." She steps up to me, running her hands up my chest.

"I'm ready to be your wife 100%. I want this life with you. I want to wake up and have coffee and breakfast with you every morning. Then, come home and have dinner with you every night. I want to have kids and fill this house with a family with you."

I wrap my arms around her and bury my face in her neck.

"I want it all, too. God, I can't wait to have kids with you. You're going to be an amazing mother."

"I'm glad to hear you say that, because... I'm pregnant." She says, and the world stops spinning. I feel it come to a crashing halt. Pulling back, I look into her eyes, and she's smiling so wide.

"I found out this morning." She says as she brings her hand up to wipe away the tears on my face that I hadn't even realized had fallen.

"I didn't think I could love you anymore, and then you go and prove me wrong," I tell her.

Then, in the next moment, I'm swooping her off her feet and carrying her to the dining room. I sit her down.

"You need to eat and drink water. Ella always says her doctor is telling her she isn't getting enough water." I reach into the fridge and pull out a bottle of water and open it for her.

"Dinner is ready to go. It's just been kept warm. Nick helped me." She says. "It's your favorite, pulled pork BBQ sandwiches. There's some coleslaw in the fridge, along with the BBQ sauce."

I'm choked up again. She really did pull out all the stops. Only she didn't have, too. Simply hearing she loves me is enough to make me the happiest man on this Earth. It's all I've ever wanted.

I serve dinner and sit down, as I pull her into my lap and make sure she eats.

"I also cornered everyone else and finally got the details of our wedding. Do you want to know?" She asks shyly.

"Of course, I want to know about the second-best day of my life that I can't remember." We both laugh.

"Well, apparently this was all a set up by my grandma. Megan thinks she knew there was alcohol in the drinks, but Ella isn't so sure. Then, I guess Nick made a joke about skipping all the wedding planning and getting married in Vegas, and you joked we should too, and my grandma egged it on." She stops to take another bite.

"We ended up at an Elvis wedding chapel, and the guys tried to talk us out of it, and the girls pushed us into it, so we got married. They swear they have photos, and they're going to send them to us."

"What about after the wedding?" I ask.

"We went for ice cream, which we both smashed in each other's faces, like the cake at a reception. Then, I was telling everyone who would listen, that it was time to commence the wedding night festivities and pulled you back to the hotel room." His face flushes.

"Well, maybe it's safe to say we did have sex." I smile.

"I think more like we got in, got undressed, and both passed out. I'm telling you when we have sex, I feel it the next day. I'm deliciously sore, and I wasn't that morning."

"Okay, fair enough. Do you want to do a vow renewal that we'll both remember and invite the town and your brother, too?"

"I'd like that. Can we do it before I start to show? I want to get wedding photos, too."

"Done."

When she finishes the first sandwich, I make her another one, and she finishes that one, too.

"Want another one?" I ask.

"I couldn't eat any more if I tried." She says, leaning back into me. Her in my arms is the most incredible feeling in the world.

I move my hand up her thigh and slowly under her dress. She spreads her legs for me, and I run my hand over her soaked underwear.

"Now that you're fed, I'm going to make love to my wife," I whisper in her ear, as I run my other hand up her thigh and under her dress.

"Yes, baby. I need you so bad." She moans.

"I know you do. I can feel it." I shift and scoop her up into my arms, carrying her to our bed.

"I love this dress. You took my breath away when I saw you tonight. But I think I'm going to love you even more out of it."

I help her out of her dress but seeing her in the black lace underwear set against her tan skin is my undoing. I lean in, running my nose down her stomach to just above the waistband of her underwear. Right where our little peanut is growing.

I place soft kisses all over her lower belly. "I love you, my little peanut, as much as I love your mom. I didn't know it was possible to love one person this much, much less two of you."

Life has a way of taking your darkest day and flipping them on their heads and leading you to the brightest days.

Epilogue

I t's funny how small your problems can seem when you're flying 30,000 feet in the air. The large clouds look like the softest cotton. It's nearly impossible to make out smaller buildings and cars.

Up here, your problems don't exist. You can't make phone calls or check social media unless you pay for the internet. And why would you pay to bring your problems here? No, up here, I can let it all go.

This is the reason flying has always given me a sense of peace. I'm flying back to Texas to spend the summer with Sage and her family before I head back for my last semester of classes to become a midwife. Then, I have to begin training under someone. I have applied to a few local places back in Arkansas, but I'm not sure that's where I want to be. I'm hoping this summer will bring clarity to the decisions I have to make in my life.

I recently started a courtship with a man, who my parents would love. The Rutherford's, who I have been staying with, love him. They were friends with my parents, and after my parents died, they were more than happy to take me in, while I went to school.

The problem is, he's everything I should want. Successful has a good job and treats me like gold, but I don't feel a single thing for him. Not even when he kisses me. I would say I could grow to love him, but there's another man who makes my heart race when he looks at me. Though, I'd never admit it to anyone.

I sigh. I want to love William, I do. I'm hoping maybe I will miss him during the summer. If not, then I guess I have my answer.

I also need to figure out where I want to finish out the rest of my schooling. I never thought of settling in Arkansas, and while the Rutherford's are nice people, I haven't really connected with anyone outside the family. I go to church every Sunday and hang out with a few girls from school, but it's nothing like the friendship Sage and I have, and I miss her like crazy. Hence, why I'm on a plane back to Texas.

I'm excited to help out around the ranch this summer, and Sage says they can use some help at the church.

At the thought of spending time at the church, my heart skips a beat. Pastor Greg is putting on the annual summer carnival and can use all the hands to help he can get. If I'm honest, I know I wouldn't mind seeing him again.

Pastor Greg is the town pastor. He's young, only a few years older than me, and he's single. A fact the church ladies in town haven't forgotten. I'm always hearing stories of how they're trying to set him up on dates.

There was a rumor going around he was dating a city girl from Dallas because he was making trips to the city at least once a week. Sage laughed at that. He was helping at a local charity, filling in for a friend, whose mom was sick, and went home to help take care of her.

As we get ready to land in Dallas, I can't help but think that it feels like coming home. I want to see if there's a way I can continue my schooling here. I haven't admitted that to anyone out loud yet. I'm scared to hope for it because there's a big chance it won't happen.

Plus, I'm not ready to have that talk with William about a long-distance relationship, if we continue.

He has all these plans for me being a stay-at-home mom to our kids, and maybe, helping out as a midwife for the church here and there. I didn't have the nerve to tell him I didn't go through all this schooling to occasionally help at a birth.

I don't see the point in fighting with him if I'm not even sure I want to continue the relationship when I get home in a few months. But he's the exact type of guy my parents would want me to settle down with, and I don't want to disappoint them.

I know they are watching over me, and I'm sure they sent William to me. There have been some signs. He likes the same music my dad did, and he has the same favorite foods as my mom. That has to mean something, right?

The plane lands, and I head to the baggage claim area, where Sage is going to meet me. I take my time and soak up all things Texas here. Dallas is a huge airport with shops, restaurants, and even complete day spas. Of course, there are all things Dallas Cowboys, too.

I'm not a Cowboys fan, but I do like to stop in one of the stores and see all the new merchandise each time I'm here. Today, everything seems to be on sale to clear out last year's inventory and get ready for the new season. I buy a key chain just something small to remember the trip. My time here is going to change the course of my life. Either I choose to continue on in Arkansas, or I make the leap and move to Texas.

Mom and Dad, if you are up there, give me a sign, which way to go.

• • • •**•**•**•**• • •

Greg

I love Rock Springs most days. I love my job as pastor here, but what I don't like is the hour before church every Sunday, where all the church ladies try to set me up with any single girl they know, who goes to church.

I know they mean well. They want me to be happy, and there's a certain responsibility a pastor's wife takes in the church, such as helping organize events. All the stuff I've been doing. I don't mind. It keeps me busy, and I know the Lord will bring that special girl to me when the timing is right.

"What about that Erin girl we met over in Lake Worth when we were helping with the charity drive?" Joy Miller says.

"Oh, yes. She was very sweet and loved helping organize the tables." Donna Norwood says.

"Mom, stop encouraging them." Hunter laughs. Hunter and his wife, Megan, have always stepped in to stop the onslaught of the church ladies, trying to set me up. They don't come to church every Sunday, and I can't blame them with a new little baby.

"Why don't you go find your seats? We will get started soon," I say and flash my biggest smile.

My dad says they wouldn't try so hard to set me up if they didn't like me, so I just keep telling myself that. I love it here in Rock Springs, and I hope to be the pastor for a good long while.

I head back to the office to get the rest of my notes when I see her. *Abby*.

I heard she was coming back for the summer. Sage even mentioned she'd be helping with the summer carnival. I wish she lived here; she's one girl I wouldn't mind getting to know better. My heart races, when she's near, and she's the one person who can make me completely lose my train of thought.

I know she's finishing classes, and I searched online for the next steps for her. She has to work with some other midwives and get hands-on experience. There definitely isn't enough of that here in our small town.

As I walk to the pulpit, the room quiets down. I go through the regular weekly announcements about volunteers for the summer carnival, who has asked for prayer requests, and some of the events in town. Then, we sing, and I give my sermon, and it all goes by in a blur because all I see is Abby. She looks like an angel sitting there in her summer dress with her hair in a braid over her shoulder.

She's sitting with Sage and Colt and their parents. They are always a reminder of what love can do for a person. Colt was very much a playboy, and while I don't know the details, I know what was said in town. I never saw him set foot in the church. Then, he and Sage got their second chance, and for her, he started coming every week. Now, he's one of my go to guys, whenever I need help to fix something around here.

Once the service is over, I stand by the door and greet everyone, thanking them for coming and chatting with whoever stops. The whole time I'm keeping an eye on Abby, who is surrounded by the church ladies. Sage is by her side, so I know she won't let them overwhelm Abby.

A smile spreads across my face remembering the first time Sage brought Colt to church, and they attended the potluck after Mrs. Dorothy Carey tried to stick her nose in like Colt didn't belong here. Sage put them all in their place that day and has walked around on Colt's arm with her head held high ever since. The next week I gave a sermon on acceptance, and how we can love the sinner but not the sin. I gave a long speech on how anyone was welcome in this church, no matter their past. Apparently, that was the speech that won Colt over.

I'm so lost in the memory and going through the motions of saying goodbye to people, that I don't realize Abby is in front of me, until the zing shoots up my arm, as she shakes my hand.

"Thanks for the sermon. I think it's just what I needed." She gives me a blinding smile.

What the heck did I give a sermon on today? I search my thoughts. Oh, how following scripture doesn't mean you have to do things that make you unhappy. It was more directed to the church ladies as a subtle hint to lay off the girl hunting for a while.

"I'm glad. I heard you were here for the summer?" I ask, wanting to talk to her, even just a bit longer.

"Yeah, I have a break in classes and missed Sage and her family, so I figured it was the perfect time to come visit. Sage signed me up to help with the summer carnival, so you'll be seeing a lot more of me. I hope you don't mind."

Mind? I'm looking forward to it.

"Sage said you had experience putting on some events with your parents' church?" I ask.

Her face clouds over for just a moment; I assume it's at the mention of her parents, who passed away last year. But the look is gone fast.

"Yeah, my mom was always involved, and I helped her a lot."

"Well, I might make you my wingman then. Donna Norwood, Hunter's mom, normally helps take the lead, but with Megan just having the baby, she has taken on fewer duties, so she can spoil her grandbaby."

"I'd like that. I'm here to help any way I can." She smiles.

Oh boy, don't make promises you can't keep. I will invent ways to keep you nearby.

This summer is starting to look up. I might not even mind the church ladies meddling if it includes Abby.

I watch her walk off with Sage and Colt, as I chuckle. Yes, this summer might be the best one yet.

· · · ● · ● ● · · ·

Want Abby and Greg's story? Grab the next book in the series!
The Cowboy and His Angel

· · · ● · ● ● · · ·

Want 2 FREE books from me? Grab these FREE Novellas by joining my newsletter!
2 Free Books From Kaci Rose
https://kacirose.com/free-books/

Connect with Kaci M. Rose

Kaci M. Rose writes steamy small town cowboys. She also writes under Kaci Rose and there she writes wounded military heroes, giant mountain men, sexy rock stars, and even more there. Connect with her below!

Website
Facebook
Kaci Rose Reader's Facebook Group
Goodreads
Book Bub
Join Kaci M. Rose's VIP List (Newsletter)

More Books by Kaci M. Rose

Rock Springs Texas Series
The Cowboy and His Runaway – Blaze and Riley
The Cowboy and His Best Friend – Sage and Colt
The Cowboy and His Obsession – Megan and Hunter
The Cowboy and His Sweetheart – Jason and Ella
The Cowboy and His Secret – Mac and Sarah
Rock Springs Weddings Novella
Rock Springs Box Set 1-5 + Bonus Content

Cowboys of Rock Springs
The Cowboy and His Mistletoe Kiss – Lilly and Mike
The Cowboy and His Valentine – Maggie and Nick

The Cowboy and His Vegas Wedding –
Royce and Anna
The Cowboy and His Angel – Abby and
Greg
The Cowboy and His Christmas Rockstar –
Savannah and Ford
The Cowboy and His Billionaire – Brice
and Kayla

Walker Lake, Texas
The Cowboy and His Beauty - Sky and
Dash

About Kaci M Rose

Kaci M Rose writes cowboy, hot and steamy cowboys set in all town anywhere you can find a cowboy.

She enjoys horseback riding and attending a rodeo where is always looking for inspiration.

Kaci grew on a small farm/ranch in Florida where they raised cattle and an orange grove. She learned to ride a four-wheeler instead of a bike (and to this day still can't ride a bike) and was driving a tractor before she could drive a car.

Kaci prefers the country to the city to this day and is working to buy her own slice of land in the next year or two!
Kaci M Rose is the Cowboy Romance alter ego of Author Kaci Rose.

See all of Kaci Rose's Books here.

Please Leave a Review!

I love to hear from my readers! Please **head over to your favorite store and leave a review** of what you thought of this book!